P9-EMO-171

"It's good to see you again...to see you looking so strong."

Strong. Not beautiful or healthy or good. Sheri liked the word. It spoke of overcoming weakness— exactly what she felt she had done. "Thank you."

A bell rang. "My lunch break is almost over," she said.

"I have to go too." He touched her arm. "Are we good now? Can we be friends?"

She hesitated. She had loved Erik more than she had loved anyone except their daughter. And she had hated him with the same depth and ferocity. Could she find a balance between the two? "I'll try," she said.

"I've never known you to give less than your full effort," he said. He kissed her cheek, a move that would surely have half the students and most of the administration who heard of it talking.

But the kiss felt good. Warm and familiar and a little thrilling.

The start of something, though she didn't want to think further than that.

CANYON KIDNAPPING

CINDI MYERS

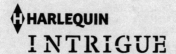

HARLEQUIN
INTRIGUE

If you purchased this book without a cover you should be aware that this book is stolen property. It was reported as "unsold and destroyed" to the publisher, and neither the author nor the publisher has received any payment for this "stripped book."

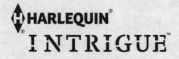

ISBN-13: 978-1-335-58229-4

Canyon Kidnapping

Recycling programs for this product may not exist in your area.

Copyright © 2022 by Cynthia Myers

All rights reserved. No part of this book may be used or reproduced in any manner whatsoever without written permission except in the case of brief quotations embodied in critical articles and reviews.

This is a work of fiction. Names, characters, places and incidents are either the product of the author's imagination or are used fictitiously. Any resemblance to actual persons, living or dead, businesses, companies, events or locales is entirely coincidental.

For questions and comments about the quality of this book, please contact us at CustomerService@Harlequin.com.

Harlequin Enterprises ULC
22 Adelaide St. West, 41st Floor
Toronto, Ontario M5H 4E3, Canada
www.Harlequin.com

Printed in U.S.A.

Cindi Myers is the author of more than fifty novels. When she's not plotting new romance story lines, she enjoys skiing, gardening, cooking, crafting and daydreaming. A lover of small-town life, she lives with her husband and two spoiled dogs in the Colorado mountains.

Books by Cindi Myers

Harlequin Intrigue

Eagle Mountain Search and Rescue

Eagle Mountain Cliffhanger
Canyon Kidnapping

Eagle Mountain: Search for Suspects

Disappearance at Dakota Ridge
Conspiracy in the Rockies
Missing at Full Moon Mine
Grizzly Creek Standoff

The Ranger Brigade: Rocky Mountain Manhunt

Investigation in Black Canyon
Mountain of Evidence
Mountain Investigation
Presumed Deadly

Eagle Mountain Murder Mystery: Winter Storm Wedding

Ice Cold Killer
Snowbound Suspicion
Cold Conspiracy
Snowblind Justice

Visit the Author Profile page at Harlequin.com.

CAST OF CHARACTERS

Sheri Stevens—The Search and Rescue volunteer and avid ice climber came to Eagle Mountain three years ago to escape a tragedy, but she's learning she can't outrun her past.

Detective Erik Lester—Erik regrets his breakup with Sheri but isn't sure the middle of a kidnapping case is the right time to try again.

Dawn Sheffield—The eight-year-old disappeared in the middle of Eagle Mountain's annual ice climbing festival.

Carl Westover—On the run from embezzlement charges, Carl demands a million dollars for the release of his niece, Dawn, but authorities suspect he isn't working alone.

Melissa Sheffield—Her daughter, Dawn, was last seen pleading to go back to her mother. Melissa is ready to pay anything for the safe return of her child.

Brandon Sheffield—The millionaire is frantic for his daughter's return, but doesn't believe caving in to Carl's demands will solve anything.

Chapter One

Climbing walls of rock or ice was all about conquering obstacles, Sheri Stevens thought as she watched competitors in the Eagle Mountain Ice Festival tackle the challenging routes up the walls of Caspar Canyon. The realization that she could face tough things that frightened her and emerge victorious had drawn her to the sport four years ago, and in that time she had grown stronger and more confident than she had ever imagined would be possible. She had learned how to carry the pain of the past without letting it defeat her.

She didn't say these things to the people who stopped by the Picksie Chix booth at the ice festival. They would discover that aspect of the sport soon enough—or not. "Climbing is terrific exercise and a lot of fun," she told the two teenage girls who approached the booth. They wore matching fake-fur-trimmed parkas and Ugg boots against the February chill. "Once you've finished a challenging climb, you'll know you can conquer anything."

"We saw you up there earlier," the taller of the two girls, a high school junior named Monica, said.

"You were amazing," her friend, Lexie, said. "Didn't you win a medal or something?"

"I'm in the running for a medal in the time trials," Sheri said. She had won her class in the annual ice climbing competition last year and hoped to repeat her victory this year. "There is another competitive climb tomorrow and exhibition climbs on Sunday."

"Good luck." Monica picked up one of the Picksie Chix brochures.

"I'm teaching a free women's climbing clinic Sunday at one," Sheri said. "You should both come."

"Maybe we will," Lexie said. "Though I don't know if my mom could handle it. She won't even come watch the other climbers, it freaks her out so much."

"Invite your mom to come with you to my clinic," Sheri said. "She can see all the safety precautions we take, and she can even try climbing herself."

Lexie wrinkled her nose. "Isn't she a little old to take up a sport like climbing?"

"I was thirty before I ever tried it," Sheri said. "And there are people in their sixties and seventies who are still climbing."

The girls looked as if they didn't believe her, but were polite enough not to say so. "Maybe we'll see you tomorrow," Monica said, and the two wandered off.

Kim Lazaro arrived to take over manning the booth.

"I saw your climb earlier," she said. "You looked great up there."

"Thanks," Sheri said. "I haven't had as much time to practice as I'd like, but I was pleased with how things went this morning."

"All that climbing you do for Search and Rescue has to help," Kim said. "From what I read in the paper, you folks have been busy this winter."

"It hasn't slowed down all year," Sheri said.

"Honestly, woman, I couldn't keep up with your schedule," Kim said. "When do you sleep?"

Sheri laughed. "I guess I'm just someone who likes to keep busy." She checked her watch. "And in a few minutes I'm due over at the Search and Rescue booth." In addition to answering questions about search and rescue, the booth volunteers handed out applications to potential volunteers and sold T-shirts to raise money for the group, which always operated on a shoestring.

She said goodbye to Kim and headed across the open area at the entrance to the canyon, where various local organizations and businesses had set up booths. She passed the booth for the local barbecue place, a big iron smoker on a trailer filling the canyon with the scent of cooking ribs and brisket. Hundreds of people filled the area, mingling among the booths or gathering closer to the base of the cliffs to watch the climbers make their way up and down the canyon walls, over flows of ice tinted pink and green and blue and orange by minerals in the water.

Sheri paused as a familiar figure—fellow SAR volunteer Eldon Ramsey—started up a route dubbed Free Style. Though relatively new to the sport, he was a good climber, and making a terrific start.

"Mommy!"

The child's shout stopped Sheri's breath and she looked around, heart pounding. A little girl raced toward her, dark hair flying out behind her. *It isn't Claire*, Sheri reminded herself, and tried to bring her breathing back under control. But this little girl was about the age Claire would be now, and seeing her sent a sharp ache through Sheri.

The little girl stopped short just a few feet from Sheri and looked up at her in obvious confusion. "I was looking for my mom," she said. She was about eight years old, with straight dark hair that hung past her shoulders, and big brown eyes fringed with black lashes.

"What's your mom's name?" Sheri asked. She looked around, hoping to spot a woman who was obviously searching for a lost child. "I'll help you find her."

"It's okay." A man hurried up and took the little girl's hand. He was about forty, with thinning brown hair and a narrow face. He wore dark aviator glasses and a blue windbreaker over tan chinos and scuffed hiking boots.

"I want my mom!" the little girl insisted, and tried to pull out of the man's grasp.

"Dawn, you need to calm down," the man said.

"I told you I'd take you to your mother, but you have to behave." He glanced up at Sheri. "Sorry about that." Then he scooped the child into his arms and walked away.

The little girl watched Sheri over the man's shoulders, her eyes brimming with tears. Sheri's own eyes burned, but she blinked rapidly to clear them. This kind of thing had happened before, but it always shook her. When she was fifty, she would probably still be seeing young women and automatically calculating if they were the same age her daughter, Claire, would have been if she had lived. She would never stop wondering what Claire would have been like at eight or eighteen or twenty-eight or forty-eight. There would come a day when no one else on earth would remember her daughter, but Sheri would never forget.

She watched the man and the girl until they disappeared in the crowd, then gathered herself and continued toward the Eagle Mountain Search and Rescue booth. She was waylaid twice, once by a fellow teacher at Eagle Mountain High School, and once by two of her students, who wanted to talk about her climb this morning. By the time she broke free she was already late for her shift at the booth, but consoled herself that the volunteer schedules were staggered, so even if the person ahead of her on the roster had to leave, someone would be there.

"I'm sorry I'm late," she said, as soon as she approached the booth, which was manned by SAR

Lieutenant Carrie Andrews and trainee Austen Morrissey. "I kept getting stopped by people who wanted to talk."

"No problem," Carrie said. "We've sold six T-shirts this morning."

"It's going to take a lot more to pay for the new vehicle the captain wants," Austen said.

"It all adds up. Plus, every one we sell is one less I have to pack up and take back to headquarters when the festival is over." Carrie looked past Sheri and smiled. "Good morning, Sheriff," she said. "Sergeant Walker."

Sheri turned to see Sheriff Travis Walker and his brother, Gage, closing in on the booth. Both men were in uniform, apparently patrolling the festival. But neither returned Carrie's smile. "How many volunteers do you have here today?" Travis asked.

Carrie looked around. "There's me and Sheri and Austen. Eldon is climbing right now and Tony is spotting for him. I think I saw Danny and Ted around somewhere. Why?"

"We've had a report of a missing little girl," Travis said. "I left the parents with Deputy Douglas and thought we could organize a search."

"Of course," Carrie said. "We can shut the booth down and I can radio whoever is here." She picked up a radio from the corner of the booth.

"Tell them the little girl is eight years old, fifty-five pounds, about fifty inches tall, with long brown hair and brown eyes," the sheriff said. "Her name is Dawn Sheffield."

The name jolted Sheri. "I think I just saw her," she said.

"Where?" Gage asked. "When?"

Sheri checked her watch. "About half an hour ago. Halfway between this booth and the one for Picksie Chix. I stopped to watch Eldon begin his climb and this little girl came running up to me. She thought I was her mom, but realized her mistake as she got closer. A man came up and promised to take her to her mother. He called her Dawn." Her stomach twisted. "I thought he was her father. He certainly acted as if he knew her, and she didn't seem afraid of him." Not afraid, just unhappy. Sheri had thought she was a typical tired kid, having a bit of a temper tantrum. Why hadn't she seen there was more to the girl's mood than that?

"What did this man look like?" Travis asked.

Sheri considered, wanting to give a clear, accurate description. "He was about forty, maybe five-ten or five-eleven, medium build, thinning brown hair. He was wearing dark glasses—aviator style—a blue windbreaker, tan chinos and hiking boots."

"Dawn's father is blond, and six-three," Gage said.

"I've already sent deputies to man the festival entrance and exits," Travis said. "But if you saw him half an hour ago, there's a good chance he's already left. In the meantime, get some of your people circulating among the crowds, looking for Dawn or the man she was with." He looked at Sheri. "I'd like you to come with me and talk to the parents. I want to find out if they know anyone who fits the description of the man you saw. Particularly anyone who might want to harm their daughter."

Sheri nodded, her mouth dry. She didn't want anything to happen to that little girl.

She especially didn't want to be the person who could have saved her, and didn't.

DETECTIVE ERIK LESTER, Colorado Bureau of Investigation, had lost all patience with Carl Westover. He had dealt with tougher crooks than Westover. He had apprehended men who were smarter than Carl, and those who were more devious. Carl wasn't tough or smart or devious—he was just annoying. He was the type of person who thought he deserved a lot more than he had ever earned. Carl thought life wasn't fair and wasted most of his time trying to shift the odds in his favor. He did this by manipulating and taking advantage of other people. He had embezzled several hundred thousand dollars from the corporation he worked for, blown the money on fancy cars and vacations, then whined to anyone who would listen about how unfairly he had been treated when he was arrested for his crimes.

Now Carl had skipped town instead of showing up for his court date and Erik had to go after him. As far as Erik was concerned, Carl was wasting his time. The man hadn't even made his pursuit very challenging. He used his credit card to purchase gas and had made a beeline for the one place he was probably sure he would find refuge—his sister's second home in Eagle Mountain, Colorado. Erik fully expected to find Carl taking it easy on his sister's sofa.

Erik didn't want to be in Eagle Mountain dealing with Carl's whiny self. But he had a job to do and he was determined to do it well. So he had made the drive from Denver over several snowy mountain passes. He would have enjoyed the winter scenery if he had been headed out on vacation, but right now the trip was one more thing to add to the list of the ways Carl had annoyed him. Midmorning on a Friday in late February found him ringing the doorbell at Melissa and Brandon Sheffield's mountain getaway, a six-thousand-square-foot chalet with breathtaking views.

No one answered the bell, so Erik knocked. Then he knocked harder. No sound of movement within the house. He moved over to a large picture window and peered inside. The massive great room appeared to be empty. A child's doll lay on the leather sofa, next to a blanket, and a coffee mug sat on the top of the wooden trunk in front of the sofa, but no fire burned in the fireplace and everything gave the appearance of being unoccupied.

Frowning, Erik turned away from the door and headed back to his car. He'd look up the number for the Sheffields and give them a call. "Are you looking for Mel and Brand?" A slim woman dressed in leggings and a puffy jacket, a yoga mat tucked under one arm, paused next to the SUV in her driveway next door. "I think they went to the ice festival. I saw them leave a little while ago."

"Do you know if Melissa's brother is visiting?" Erik asked. "I was hoping to talk to him."

The woman shook her head, blond ponytail swaying. "I don't think so. It was just the two of them and their little girl when they left this morning."

"Thanks." Erik got into his car and pulled away before the woman could ask who he was and what he wanted with Melissa's brother. Not that he couldn't lie with the best of them but it was easier to avoid awkward questions in the first place.

He was wondering how he'd find out where the ice festival was when he spotted a large banner hanging over the street as he entered Eagle Mountain. "Welcome to the thirtieth annual Ice Festival," it proclaimed. "Caspar Canyon, February 25–27." His Toyota's GPS obligingly provided directions to Caspar Canyon.

He saw the crowd for the festival long before he saw the canyon itself. The road was lined with cars, and adjacent fields had been turned into parking lots. The turnoff to the canyon was closed, and a uniformed officer directed him to turn around and park in a lot. Erik thought of flashing his badge and announcing that he was looking for a fugitive, but that was a good way to panic people needlessly. The last thing he wanted was for Carl to have any warning that Erik was here. With luck, the two of them would have a quiet conversation and Erik would lead Carl back to his vehicle and they'd be on their way. He had handcuffs if he needed to use them, but it would be easier on everyone if he didn't have to. Carl had no history of violence. He was a dishonest man, but he had never physically hurt anyone, so Erik didn't expect trouble.

Metal gates blocked off the entrance to the canyon and people were lined up waiting to enter. Beyond the entrance, he could see vendors' booths and a glimpse of high rock walls coated in ice, ropes dangling from the ice, and people dangling from the ropes. He estimated the crowd in his view at a couple of hundred people, with more farther into the canyon. He hoped he wouldn't have too much trouble tracking down the Sheffields, and after that, locating Carl.

The line he was in wasn't moving. "What's going on?" a man behind him asked.

"They're not letting people in," a woman beside him answered. "The cops have closed it down."

Erik made his way to the front of the line, ignoring disgruntled remarks from a few people he passed. He approached a man in a sheriff's department uniform and held up his badge. "What's going on, Deputy?" he asked.

"A little girl has gone missing," the man, whose name badge identified him as Deputy Doyle, said. "We're not letting anyone in or out while we search for her and the man who may have taken her."

"How old a child?" Erik asked. "What does she look like?"

"She's eight. Long dark hair and brown eyes. Her name is Dawn Sheffield."

Erik felt cold all over. He didn't believe it was a coincidence that the Sheffields' daughter had gone missing at the same time Melissa Sheffield's brother was fleeing criminal charges and known to be headed this way. In his experience, crimes like this were always connected. "I might have information that could help," Erik said. "Could someone take me to the Sheffields?"

He had thought Carl was too dumb to be a real danger to anyone, but maybe Erik was the one who wasn't so smart. He, of all people, ought to know that danger could lurk in the most unexpected places, and not realizing that could lead to the worst of all consequences.

SHERIFF WALKER AND Gage escorted Sheri to the first aid tent, where a couple sat with Deputy Jamie Douglas. The woman, her dark hair cut in an asymmetrical style that set off her elfin features, stood when they entered the tent. "Have you found her?" she asked.

Travis shook his head. "This is Sheri Stevens," he said. "She saw a girl we think may be Dawn. Sheri, this is Brandon and Melissa Sheffield."

"Where was this?" Brandon Sheffield, a tall, broad-shouldered blond who looked as if he'd be more at home in a logging camp than a boardroom, turned eagerly to Sheri. "Was she all right? Was she afraid?"

"The child I saw was asking for her mother, but otherwise she seemed fine." Sheri chose her words carefully. She wanted to tell the truth, but she didn't want to upset this mother and father any more than she could help. "She was a very pretty little girl, with long dark hair, parted in the middle, and big brown eyes. She was with a man with thinning brown hair. He called her Dawn and she seemed to know him, though I never heard her address him by name."

"That sounds like Dawn," Brandon said. "And Carl." He turned to his wife. "Don't you think that sounds like Carl?"

"Who is Carl?" Gage asked.

"My wife's brother," Brandon said. "Dawn wouldn't be afraid of him. To her, he's just her uncle."

"Why would your brother take Dawn without your knowing about it?" Travis asked Melissa.

"He wouldn't." She looked up at her husband. "Brand, I'm sure you're wrong. Carl wouldn't do something like that."

Brandon ignored her protest and turned to the officers. "Carl is in trouble for embezzling money from his former employer," he said. "He asked me for one hundred thousand dollars to pay his legal fees and when I refused, he got angry. Maybe he took Dawn to get back at me."

"No. My brother wouldn't do something like that," Melissa said. "And the whole business with the money—it was just a misunderstanding. I don't know why you wouldn't give him the money he needed. He would have paid me back."

"Right. Like he paid back the money I lent him to buy his last house, or the loan you gave him before we were married."

Watching these two argue made Sheri's stomach hurt. They were both afraid and hurting, but instead of coming together to present a united front, they were already pulling away. She wanted to tell them to stop it—they didn't realize the damage they were doing. She knew too well how easy it was to blame the person you were closest to for all the pain you were feeling—and how the damage hurtful words inflicted could never be undone.

But she was a stranger to these people. The last thing they wanted was advice from her, especially when the counsel came in the form of "don't make the same mistake I did."

"Do you have a picture of your brother?" Travis asked.

"Not with me," Melissa said.

"I think I do." Brandon took out his phone. "I took a lot of pictures when we were all together at Melissa's parents' place last Christmas." He swiped through several photos, then angled the phone toward them. "Carl is the one in the middle, next to Melissa."

Sheri stared at the man in the photo. He was smiling,

and looked a little younger, but it was the same man. "That's the man I saw with the little girl," she said.

Brandon turned the phone toward himself and scrolled once more. "Is this the little girl you saw?" he asked, and showed her a photograph of a smiling child, her long dark hair whipped by a breeze, dressed in shorts and a T-shirt, on the deck of a boat.

Sheri nodded. "Yes, that's her."

Melissa Sheffield began to cry, and sank into a chair. Brandon hesitated, then put his arm around his wife. "It's going to be okay," he said. "Now that we know who has Melissa, we can find him. He can't have gone far in such a short time."

"I'm sure Carl would never hurt Dawn," Melissa said. "He loves her."

"I don't think Carl is violent," Brandon said. "He's greedy and manipulative, but he's not violent. And he does love Dawn."

Melissa pulled away from her husband. "Carl is not greedy and manipulative," she said. "He hasn't had the same advantages you've had and people always underestimate him."

"Do you have any idea where your brother might have taken Dawn?" Travis asked. "A friend's house? Someplace else he's frequented?"

"We're the only people he knows here," Melissa said.

The sheriff turned to Sheri. "What, exactly, did he say when you saw him?" he asked.

She relayed as much as she could remember of the brief exchange. "He told the little girl he was going to take her to her mother. But he didn't say where or when."

"What kind of vehicle does your brother drive?" Gage asked.

"The last time I saw him, he had a Lexus, I think?" Melissa looked to her husband for confirmation.

"He drives a Lexus LS. Black," Brandon said. "Or he did last month. He leases vehicles and switches them out pretty often."

"When was the last time you spoke to your brother, Mrs. Sheffield?" Travis asked.

"A few days ago. We talk and text regularly. He was getting ready for his trial and he seemed in good spirits."

"He was out on bail and was upset I wouldn't give him the money he wanted," Brandon said. "Apparently, he'd already blown the money he stole on fancy vacations and new suits and no telling what else."

"He didn't steal any money!" Melissa protested.

"Did he make any threats to you or your wife, when you refused to give him the money?" Travis asked.

"No!" Melissa jumped up again. "You're making him sound like some hardened criminal and he isn't. If Dawn is with Carl, I'm sure he'll bring her back to us soon."

"He whined about me not having any faith in him, but he didn't make threats," Brandon said. He looked at his wife. "I hope you're right. All I want is for Dawn to be safe."

"I don't believe he did this," Melissa said. She turned to Sheri. "You may have seen Dawn with Carl, but that doesn't mean Carl took her anywhere. Maybe he really was taking her to me, but before he could find me, someone else intercepted them. Or maybe Dawn ran away, Carl lost track of her in the crowd and someone else took her."

"Then why didn't he come to us and tell us what happened?" Brandon asked.

"Because he knew you'd accuse him of doing something awful. You've never liked him and he knows it."

"Did your brother mention he was coming to see you?" Gage asked.

Melissa shook her head, and hugged her arms over her chest. "Carl is family. He doesn't have to wait for an invitation to come see me. He's always welcome. He probably wanted to surprise me."

"Have you tried calling him?" Travis asked.

Brandon took out his phone again. "There's no signal down here in this canyon."

"When you get to someplace with a signal, I want you to call him," Travis said. "If you reach him, please ask him to stop by the sheriff's department and give a statement."

"Of course," Melissa said. "I'm sure he'll want to do everything he can to help." She shook her head.

"But I can't believe the man you saw really was Carl. Lots of men have brown hair."

"Carl Westover is here, all right."

They all turned to look at the man who spoke— a tall, dark-haired man with olive skin and a strong jaw. Sheri stared at him, dizzy and disoriented.

He stared back, eyes burning into hers. "Sheri!" He didn't try to hide his shock at seeing her. "What are you doing here?"

"I live here." The words came out with more force than she intended. She worked to rein in her agitation. "What are you doing here, Erik?"

Erik looked at the others, and fixed on the sheriff. He held out his hand. "Detective Erik Lester, Colorado Bureau of Investigation," he introduced himself.

"Sheriff Travis Walker." The sheriff shook Erik's hand, then examined the credentials he offered.

"I'm here because I've been tracking Carl Westover ever since he jumped bail and failed to appear for his trial yesterday," Erik said. "His credit card receipts showed he was headed to Eagle Mountain, I presumed to visit his sister." He looked to Melissa. "Carl didn't tell you he was coming?"

"No. I already told these people that."

"I stopped by the Sheffields' house before I came here," Erik said. "I didn't see any sign of Carl and the neighbor I talked to hadn't seen him."

"He was seen approximately forty-five minutes ago with his niece," Travis said.

"Who saw him?" Erik said. "I'd like to talk to them."

"I saw him," Sheri said. She really couldn't believe this was happening. Erik was the last person she wanted to talk to.

"Do you two know each other?" Gage asked.

Sheri stood up straighter, her eyes fixed on Erik. "You could say that," she said. "Erik is my ex-husband."

Chapter Two

Seeing Sheri again had shaken Erik more than he wanted to admit. Of all the people he would have gone out of his way to avoid running into, her name was at the top of the list. Not because he didn't want to face her—he wouldn't have minded keeping in touch after their divorce, but she had insisted on a clean break. Just another way she had rejected him.

He pulled back from the silent criticism. He had done his share of ugly things in the last couple of years of their marriage. There was plenty of blame to go around on all sides. At the time she had made her statement about wanting a clean break, he had put it down to her attempt to cope with Claire's death by making a fresh start. He had even agreed that might be a good idea.

Seeing her now, he was struck by how much she looked the same—and how different she was. She was thinner, but not skinny. There was a lot of muscle definition in the arms showing in her tight Lycra shirt and the thighs beneath purple athletic leggings.

She looked fit and healthy. She had cut her hair short, and though he had always loved her long blond hair, the new style suited her. He could still read the pain in her eyes when she met his gaze, but maybe that was only because he knew her so well. Or at least he had, once upon a time.

"What did Carl look like when you saw him?" he asked. Keeping their focus on the business at hand was the best way to get through the awkwardness, he thought. "What was he wearing?"

Nothing stood out about the outfit she described. "You're wasting your time looking for Carl." Melissa Sheffield stood. "He wouldn't hurt Dawn—I know he wouldn't. Meanwhile, whoever did take her is getting farther and farther away."

"Do you know of anyone else who might take your daughter?" Travis asked. "Someone with a grudge against you? A business rival? A disgruntled employee? Has anyone made threats against you?"

"No." Brandon Sheffield shook his head. Erik had met him only once before, but Sheffield had struck him as smart—and someone who saw his brother-in-law for the con man he was, despite his wife's rosy view of her younger brother. "No one has made threats—not against me, or my daughter."

"We have dozens of people from the sheriff's department and with the local search and rescue organization looking for your daughter," Travis said. "We've issued an Amber Alert for a missing child, which goes out to other law enforcement agencies and transportation companies. Now that we have a good description of Dawn and of your brother we'll share that information as well. There's a good chance someone will see them."

Erik was sure Melissa was going to protest again that her brother hadn't taken Dawn, but at a look from her husband she merely pressed her lips together and nodded.

A big blond sheriff's deputy joined them. "We've searched the entire canyon and no one reports seeing the little girl—either by herself or with someone else," he said. "No one has entered or left since we shut down the entrance, but people are starting to complain."

Travis nodded. "Open things back up, but keep a couple of deputies on the entrance, just in case whoever has the girl managed to evade the searchers and tries to slip out."

"There's a photographer from the paper here and he's agreed to share all the crowd photos he took, and there's a guy here with a drone who's been filming a competition," the deputy said. "He's agreed to turn over copies of all his footage. Oh, and Tony Meisner, the SAR captain, wants to talk to you. He thinks he saw the girl over by the restroom, a little before she was reported missing."

"Where is Tony now?" Gage asked.

"He's at the SAR tent." The deputy pointed in the direction of the exhibitors. "He said he would wait for you there."

Travis nodded. "Good thinking on the photos and video," he said. He turned to Sheri. "We'll need you to come by the station and give us a formal statement."

"Of course," she said. "Anything I can do to help."

"Mr. and Mrs. Sheffield, you can return to your home," Travis said to the couple. "We'll let you know if we hear anything about your daughter. We'll send a deputy with you, to check for any sign of your brother."

Again, Erik thought Melissa would object, but her husband cut her off. "Of course. Whatever you need to do."

"Someone at the station will take your statement when you're ready," Gage told Sheri. He looked at Erik. "It would be helpful if you'd share what you know about Carl Westover."

"Of course."

The officers and the Sheffields left. Sheri turned away also, but Erik followed. "Which way did Carl and the girl head when they left you?" he asked.

"I don't know," she said. "I wasn't paying attention."

"I don't believe that. You always pay attention. Especially when a child is involved."

Because the one time she hadn't, a tragedy had happened. Sheri had never been able to forgive herself for that brief lapse, no matter how many times Erik and others told her Claire's death wasn't her fault. Accidents happened all the time, for no reason.

The glare she directed at him definitely wasn't friendly or forgiving. Fine. She hated his guts. He still had a job to do. "Which direction?" he prodded.

She halted and closed her eyes. "They headed toward the entrance," she said. "He was carrying the little girl—Dawn. She wasn't fighting him, but she didn't look happy. I thought she was just a tired child having a little tantrum. I thought he was taking her to her mother."

She was blaming herself for something she had no control over, the same way she had done after Claire's death. She probably wouldn't listen to him now, any more than she had then, but he had to try to steer her thoughts in another direction. "Anyone would have thought that," Erik said. "If I didn't know Carl, I would have thought that."

"What kind of man is he?" she asked. "Would he hurt her? Her mother says not, but maybe that's just because she can't bear to think the worst of her brother."

"He's never been violent before," Erik said. "He was accused of embezzling a lot of money. It's not a victimless crime, but it is nonviolent. There's nothing in his past that would indicate to me he would hurt a child, especially a family member. From what you described, Dawn wasn't afraid of him."

"She wasn't," Sheri said. She put her fist to her mouth and shook her head. "But what if we're wrong?" Tears gleamed in her eyes. Erik fought the urge to put his arm around her and pull her close. He had a feeling she wouldn't welcome the gesture.

"Don't focus on the worst possible outcome," he said. "Carl is a self-centered jerk, but so far all he's done is spirit his niece away from her parents. He could be waiting back at the house for them right now."

She nodded and took a deep breath. "This is just hard for me. Dawn is the same age Claire would be now."

"I realize that," he said. "Did you think I didn't?"

"I don't know what you think or feel," she said. "You never would tell me."

Just like that, they'd gone back in time four years, sniping at each other in a game of "he said, she said" no one could ever win. "Where are you going now?" he asked.

"To the sheriff's department, to give my statement. Not that it's any concern of yours."

"Of course not." Except that he was concerned. A piece of paper said they were no longer married, and they hadn't set eyes on each other in two years, but part of him still thought of her as his wife. He would never admit it to anyone, and he knew they'd never get back together. But even though he didn't like to talk about his feelings, he could acknowledge he had them. And right now, standing close enough to her to touch, inhaling the soft scent of her and feeling her pain like fingernails tearing at his insides, he knew that divorce hadn't excised that part of his heart. "Go on, then," he said. "But I'll need to talk to you later."

She waved her hand in a gesture that could have

meant "fine" or "goodbye" or "good riddance" as she moved away from him. *It was good to see you*, he wanted to say, though he doubted she would agree.

AFTER ERIK LEFT SHERI, he went in search of the Search and Rescue booth. He found Sheriff Walker and his sergeant there with a tall, thin man with streaks of silver in his thick, dark hair. They looked up at his approach. "This is Detective Lester, with the Colorado Bureau of Investigation," Walker said by way of introduction. "And this is Tony Meisner, captain of Eagle Mountain Search and Rescue. He saw Dawn Sheffield with a man shortly before Sheri ran into them."

"Do you mind repeating what you told the sheriff?" Erik asked.

"There's not a lot to tell," Meisner said. "I was on my way to the men's room when I saw a little girl playing on the picnic tables right next to the portable toilets. She was climbing up and down the tables, the way kids do. I only noticed her because my nephew broke his arm doing just that. I looked around for a parent and spotted a man watching her. I was about to go up to him and suggest what she was doing was dangerous when he called to her. The little girl looked up, smiled at him and ran to him and put her arms around him. She certainly wasn't upset or afraid. I figured he was her dad." He looked to the deputies. "She definitely knew who this guy was."

"What did the man look like?" Erik asked.

Meisner described Carl Westover to a T, including the Western Casing logo on the left side of the windbreaker he wore—a detail Sheri had missed. "Western Casing was the company Carl Westover worked for," Erik said.

"I know I would have recognized the man and the girl if I had seen them again when we searched the canyon," Tony said. "They must have already left by the time the alarm was raised."

"I'm sure once Carl had the girl, he got out of here as soon as possible," Erik said.

"I can't believe the only two people who remember seeing them are with Search and Rescue," Tony said. "Maybe it's just that we're trained to assess situations."

"Sheri is with Search and Rescue?" Erik asked.

"She's our training officer this year," Tony said. "A terrific volunteer. One of our best climbers."

Erik tried to connect this picture with the woman he had known. Sheri had always been fit, but never what he would call athletic. "You mean rock climbing?" he asked.

"Rocks, ice—she's really good," Tony said. "She's competing this weekend and will probably take a medal. Every volunteer trains for climbing work—it's pretty much required, working in these mountains or canyons—but if I need someone who's fearless and technically very proficient, Sheri is my go-to. And she's a great training officer. Very patient and encouraging."

Fearless. Patient. Encouraging. Not the first words Erik thought of when it came to Sheri. But he supposed four years could change a person. A few seconds could change a person, if those seconds resulted in tragedy.

The sheriff told Meisner he could go, then motioned for Erik to follow him away from the booth. "If you've been following Westover, you know him better than we do," Travis said. "What do you think he's up to?"

"His sister said he asked her husband for money," Erik said. "Brandon Sheffield owns a computer software company that's worth millions. Carl is one of these people who think the world owes him. He did a lousy job of covering his tracks when he embezzled from Western Casing, but he's continued to deny stealing the money, while at the same time whining about how he wasn't paid what he was worth and was owed bonuses he never received, etc., etc. He might have taken the girl intending to force the Sheffields to pay his legal fees."

"Why does he need money for his legal fees if he stole a bunch from his employer?" Sergeant Walker—who must be the sheriff's brother, they looked enough alike—asked.

"He blew all the money he stole on vacations, wine, dinner out—who knows," Erik said. "But he doesn't have anything left."

"So we wait for some kind of ransom note," Gage said.

"We don't wait," Travis said. "We keep looking.

But I won't be surprised if the Sheffields hear from him very soon. He may try to make it look like someone else took the girl, but the more I hear, the more I think it's him."

"I think so, too," Erik said.

"When were you and Sheri married?" Gage asked.

His marriage wasn't something Erik ever talked about, but after Sheri's dramatic announcement, the questions were bound to come. "We split a couple of years ago."

"About the time she moved to Eagle Mountain," Gage said. "I went out with her a couple of times before I got married and she never mentioned an ex. Then again, we didn't date that long."

"Is she dating anyone now?" Erik regretted the question as soon as he asked it. Sheri's personal life was none of his business.

"Not that I know of," Gage said. "And it's hard to keep a secret like that around here. I know a couple of guys who were interested, but she turned a cold shoulder. Then again, she's pretty involved in Search and Rescue and she teaches high school. That probably doesn't leave much time for a social life."

Erik didn't like the way something inside him relaxed when he learned Sheri was unattached. He had never been the possessive type and he had zero claim on Sheri now. He ought to be wishing she had found someone and was happy.

"I'd appreciate it if you'd share your file on Westover," Travis said. "Do you plan on sticking around for a while?"

"I'm here until Westover is arrested," Erik said. "Even if he didn't kidnap his niece, he's a fugitive and my job is to haul him back to Denver for his trial." He pulled out his wallet, removed a business card and passed it to the sheriff. "There's my contact information. Call me anytime. And let me know if there's anything I can do to help."

"Where are you staying?" Travis asked.

"I don't know. I just got to town. I was hoping to pick up Westover at his sister's house and head straight back to Denver, but no such luck."

"The Ranch Motel on the highway is clean," Travis said. "If you wanted something fancier, there are a few bed-and-breakfasts in town. The Alpiner is good, though with the ice festival, they're probably booked up. The local real estate office keeps a list of private vacation rentals, too."

"I'll try the real estate office. I prefer something private." And he had no idea how long he would be in town.

He said goodbye to the officers and made his way through the crowd toward the mouth of the canyon. He stopped to watch a woman climbing up what looked to him to be a sheet of ice. Sheri did that— and was good at it? How had he been married to her for six years and never known that side of her?

He was going to be in Eagle Mountain a little while longer. Maybe he should take the opportunity to get to know his ex-wife better. Not with a view of getting back together—they were long past that point. But they had spent six years together, and they had shared a child, and they would always share the grief over that child's death. When they parted ways again, it was nice to think they could do so on better terms.

SHERI'S CLIMB ON the second day of competition was up a route called Snakebite, a long, steep climb navigating a tricky column of ice. After yesterday's climb she was second in the standings and had a good chance to take the lead—if she didn't let her unexpected reunion with Erik mess with her head.

She had spent more than an hour at the sheriff's department late yesterday, going over everything she could remember about those few moments with Dawn and her uncle. Erik hadn't been there, but she kept replaying the shock of seeing him again. He had looked good—even more handsome than she remembered him, lean and edgy. She had been attracted to him from the moment they met, in a gym near the school where she had been doing her student teaching in a suburb of Denver. She had fallen for him so hard—and the falling-out had been just as hard. Having him step back into her life after all this time was such a shock. She hadn't slept well, her mind racing with thoughts of Erik, and Claire, and a life that seemed so distant now.

But strong coffee and a long hot shower had put

those memories back into the box where they belonged. Today she was going to put her ex-husband out of her mind and focus on the ice. She double-checked all of her equipment and mentally ran through the climb, picturing herself making each move, each placement of her hands and feet, all the way up the ice.

"Good luck!" Her fellow Picksie Chix member Susie Fellini rushed up to hug her. "You're going to do great!" Susie said.

Then it was time. Sheri started up, all her focus on the ice and the movements she had made so many times they were instinctual—place her foot here, reach her hand up there, clip into a piton, shift her weight, lean and stretch. Sink one ax in, then the next. The cold seeped into her, but the exertion of the climb warmed her. The noise of the crowd below receded as she climbed higher and calm flooded her. This was what climbing gave her, this sense of peace and control.

Then she was at the top, the announcer giving her time as 13.260. Triumph surged through her and she thrust her arms into the air. For now, at least, she led the standings for women.

Friends and spectators she didn't know gathered to offer their congratulations. "I'm impressed." The deep, resonant voice brought her up short and she turned to find Erik standing just behind her. Had he really come to see her climb? The thought sent an unwelcome flutter through her.

"I only caught part of it, but you looked like you knew what you were doing," he said.

As compliments went, it wasn't up there with "you were amazing" but Erik had never been overly effusive. "I'm happy with the climb," she said. "If you'd like to see more, I'm doing an exhibition climb tomorrow, the last day of the festival. You should come."

"I'd like that," he said. "What time are you climbing?"

"One o'clock." Prime time, when all the various winners would be on display, as it were, for the crowds who gathered within the canyon and along the rim.

"I'll be there," he said.

"Good." Suddenly, she really wanted him to see her—to see what she was capable of. When they had last been together, she had been so broken. She wanted him to know she was past that. She would never fully heal—how could you heal from the loss of a child?—but she was alive, and doing well. No one gave medals for that kind of victory, but having Erik see all she had accomplished would be its own reward.

"I stopped by because you need to come to the sheriff's department and look at some photographs," he said.

So much for thinking his presence here was about anything but work. "I'm a little busy right now," she said, and began gathering up her gear.

"When you're done, then."

"Why didn't they ask me to do this yesterday when I was giving my statement?" she asked.

"It just came up."

"Why are you telling me this, instead of a deputy?"

"They've asked me to help with the investigation."

She said nothing, but squatted to unbuckle her crampons.

"I hear you're on the Search and Rescue squad," Erik said.

She glared at him. She did not want to make conversation with him. "Does that have anything to do with your case?" she asked.

His expression was unreadable. And to think that once upon a time she had believed she knew him so well. "I'll see you at the sheriff's department later," he said, then turned and left.

"Who was that man you were talking to after your climb?" Susie intercepted Sheri as she trudged toward the parking lot, laden with gear.

"Just somebody I used to know," Sheri said.

"A really good-looking somebody. Is he a climber?"

"No." Erik ran and lifted weights, but those were things he did to keep in shape for his job, not because he enjoyed them the way she enjoyed climbing.

"Too bad."

"What do you mean?"

"Oh, you know—if you try to have a relationship with a nonclimber, they end up complaining about all the time you spend climbing," Susie said. "They just don't get it. You've been there, right?"

"Yeah, that is a problem," Sheri said. Actually, she hadn't dated anyone seriously since she had started climbing, so she had no idea if what Susie said was true or not. She had tried to meet new men, and had even gone on a few outings to dinner or the movies, but nothing had clicked, and at last she had given up trying. She wasn't comfortable letting anyone get that close.

They reached her car and Susie helped Sheri load her gear. "Are you coming to the party tonight?" Susie asked. Saturday night of the festival always featured a big bash at the Elks Lodge.

"I don't know," Sheri said. "I have other stuff I need to do first."

"I sort of agreed to meet this Swedish climber and his friends," Susie said. "They're really cute. I could introduce you."

Sheri forced a smile. "Maybe." She wasn't in a partying mood, but she didn't want to waste time debating with Susie, who would try to change her mind.

"I promise if you show up it will be worth it," Susie said. "These guys are hot—and smart. One of them is a physicist."

Sheri waved goodbye and pulled out of the lot. She wanted to go home, take a long hot shower, then climb into bed and surrender to the dark mood that had haunted her since little Dawn Sheffield had disappeared. Which was the exact last thing she should allow herself to do. Instead, she turned her car toward the sheriff's department. She might as well get her next encounter with Erik over with.

She relaxed a little when Deputy Jamie Douglas came out to greet her in the lobby of the sheriff's department. But her hope that she'd been saved from talking to Erik was dashed when Jamie escorted her to a room where Sheriff Travis Walker and Erik waited.

Both men stood as she entered the room. "Thank you for stopping by," Travis said. "This won't take long."

The three of them sat at a plain metal table in a gray-walled room that was the very definition of drab. Erik sat across from her, a manila folder in front of him. "I'm going to lay out six photographs," he said. "I want to know if any of them is the man you saw with the little girl yesterday."

"I already identified Carl from the photo Mr. Sheffield showed me yesterday," Sheri said.

"We want to be certain of the identification," Travis said. "If you don't see the man who was with Dawn in the photo array, we want to know that, too."

She waited while he laid out the photos in a line in front of her, like a dealer in a casino. She took her time studying the images. All the men were similar, middle-aged with thinning brown hair. When she came to the fourth photograph, she felt a jolt of recognition. This image was different from the photograph Brandon Sheffield had showed her on his phone—the man in this picture was scowling, less well-dressed, but she was sure he was the same man she had seen with the little girl yesterday. Still, she made herself consider the other two images as well.

Then she sat back and pointed to the fourth photo. "That one," she said. "That's the man I saw."

"Are you sure?" Erik asked.

"Yes, I'm sure."

Erik gathered up the photos. "Thank you."

"Is that the uncle?" she asked. "The man they think took Dawn?"

"I'm not at liberty—" began Erik.

"Yes," said Travis. At least he wasn't going to shut her out. Then again, Erik had had plenty of practice excluding her from what he knew or felt.

Jamie reappeared in the doorway. "Mr. and Mrs. Sheffield are here and asking to see you, Sheriff," she said.

Travis started to stand, but Melissa Sheffield pushed past Jamie into the room, followed by her husband. "Carl texted fifteen minutes ago," she said. "He has Dawn. I can't believe he has Dawn."

Chapter Three

Melissa Sheffield's anguish filled the small room, its sharpness a physical sensation to Sheri. Memory of that feeling flooded her. She wanted to look away from such suffering, but could not.

"What did your brother say, exactly?" Erik's voice, firm yet calm, cut through the hysteria that seemed to Sheri to shimmer around Melissa.

Melissa bit her lip, then thrust the phone at him. He took it, glanced at the screen, then read out loud: "'I have Dawn. She's fine, but if you want her to stay that way, transfer one million dollars to this account now. CH86000000111.'" Erik looked up. "That sounds like a Swiss bank account. Does your brother have a Swiss account?"

"I don't know anything about that," she said.

"Are you sure Carl sent that text?" Travis asked.

"It's from his number," Melissa said.

Erik scrolled down the phone screen. "You didn't answer him?"

"No. Brand thought we should come here first."

She turned to her husband. "But we have to send him the money."

"That's ridiculous." Brandon frowned at Erik and Travis. "You can use this text to find him, can't you?" he asked.

"If you had paid him the money he asked for before, this wouldn't have happened," Melissa said.

Brandon winced. "Melissa..." he began.

She turned away. "Carl must be desperate to do this," she said. "I know he wouldn't hurt Dawn, but what if the stress has made him snap? What if he isn't in his right mind? You have to do something."

"Have you had any other communication from Carl?" Erik asked.

"No," she said.

"No," Brandon echoed.

"It's only been twenty-six hours since he was seen at the ice park," Erik said. "No one has reported seeing him and the Amber Alert has been widely distributed. I think that's an indication that he went to ground very quickly. Is there any place near here where he might hide—a vacation home or a friend's place?"

"I can't think of any place," Melissa said.

"Our house is the only place he's ever stayed in the area," Brandon said. He sent a worried look to his wife. "What if we pretend we want to pay the money, but we insist on paying in cash? We could arrange a meeting."

"Yes!" Melissa clutched his arm. "We could insist he bring Dawn and exchange her for the money."

"We could try," Erik said. "Do you think he would fall for it?"

"He wants the money," she said. "He doesn't really want Dawn."

"He might suspect a trap," Travis said.

"At least some of the money should be real," Melissa said. "If he sees that he'll be more likely to cooperate."

"He doesn't deserve a dime," Brandon said.

"We're talking about our daughter!"

"Are you saying I don't care about Dawn?"

"Stop!" Sheri hadn't meant to vent her frustration out loud, but seeing these two tear at each other when so much was at stake was too much to bear. Aware that everyone was staring at her now, she pushed on. "Your daughter needs both of you," she said. "The two of you will be stronger together than you could ever be apart."

Melissa stared, and Sheri was sure she was going to tell her to mind her own business. Sheri wouldn't blame her if she did. Instead, after a moment Melissa turned to her husband. "I'm sorry," she said. "I'm just so upset."

Brandon caressed his wife's shoulders. "I know."

Erik returned the phone to Melissa. "Send a reply," he said. "Tell him you'll give him the money. Tell him… Tell him your husband doesn't want to give it to him, but you'll liquidate some assets and bring him the cash without Brandon knowing about it. That can be your excuse for not wiring the money to a bank. Do you think he'll believe that?"

"Yes. He'll know Brandon won't want to pay him. And Carl knows I have some stocks in my name. Not a million dollars, but he doesn't know that."

"Good," Erik said. "Send him the text."

They fell silent, the tap of her nails on the screen of the phone the only sound. She hit Send and looked up. "What do we do now?" she asked.

"Now, we wait," Erik said.

As PHYSICALLY TOUGH as she might be now, Sheri was still as emotionally transparent as ever, Erik thought as he watched her observe the Sheffields snipe at each other. He knew as well as he had known anything that Sheri was reliving all the arguments the two of them had had in the months and years following Claire's death. They'd been like two warring planets sharing an orbit, unable to keep from colliding over and over. They should have been united by their shared pain, but their methods of coping with that pain had caused them to clash. He had known as well as she had that it was wrong, but neither of them could stop themselves.

When she had called on the Sheffields to come together for the sake of their daughter, Erik wondered if she wished someone had said the same thing to the two of them. Would it have made any difference? Or did how a couple reacted to stress show the true nature of their relationship? He and Sheri had started off great together, but maybe they were never really all that compatible in the first place. When faced with a real trial, their marriage had crumbled. Maybe losing Claire had only hastened the inevitable.

"I'd better go." Sheri pushed back from the table and stood.

"We'll be in touch if we have more questions," Erik said.

She nodded, not looking at him, and hurried from the room.

Melissa Sheffield sat in the chair Sheri had vacated. She held her phone, staring at the screen as if willing it to display a new message. "How are we going to fake a million dollars in cash?" Brandon Sheffield asked.

"We'll figure that out once we arrange the meeting," the sheriff said. "Tell him you'll need time to gather up the cash."

The phone in Melissa's hand buzzed and she almost dropped it. "It's Carl!" she yelped, and fumbled to unlock the screen. She stared at the message in silence, then tossed the phone on the table. "He says no." She swiveled to face her husband, who stood, back against the wall. "He says it has to be a transfer to that bank account and it has to come from you. You have to pay him. It's the only way to get Dawn back."

"And what happens after I pay him?" Brandon

straightened. "How do we even know he'll give Dawn back to us, unharmed?"

"Carl would never hurt Dawn," Melissa said.

"Then why did he kidnap her? Why is he threatening her?"

"Because he's desperate and you gave him no choice!" She started crying, hiccupping, ugly sobs that made Erik look away.

Brandon had looked away from his wife, too. He caught Erik's eye. "I want my daughter back safe," he said. "And I'd do anything to save her. But Carl has been leeching off me ever since Melissa and I got married. No matter what I give him, it's never enough. If I give him a million today, what's to keep him for asking for two million next time?"

"I agree you shouldn't pay the ransom," Erik said. "Especially not without a guarantee that Dawn will be returned to you unharmed."

Another loud sob broke from Melissa. Brandon moved closer. "Is there any way to trace his location from those texts?" he asked the sheriff.

"We'll ask his service provider to try," Travis said. "But that can be tough to do even in cities with lots of towers. The rugged terrain around here presents more challenges."

Melissa wiped at her eyes and picked up her phone again. "What should I tell Carl?" she asked.

"Tell him to call you," Erik said. "Tell him you can't send the money until you're sure that Dawn is all right. Tell him you want to talk to your daughter."

"Yes!" She began typing. "I do want to talk to Dawn. Poor baby. She must be terrified."

"Tell him if he hurts one hair on my little girl's head I will personally rip him apart with my bare hands," Brandon said.

"I will tell him so such thing." She finished typing and hit Send.

"We're contacting every hotel, motel, campground and other lodging within a two-hundred-mile radius," Travis said.

"I checked with my office," Erik said. "He hasn't used his credit cards. Do you know if he had any cash with him?"

Melissa shook her head. "I hadn't talked to him since last week, when he called to ask for money to pay his legal bills."

"If he only wanted a hundred thousand then, why is he asking for a million dollars now?" Erik asked.

"Because Carl never has enough," Brandon said. "And he's angry that I refused to give him the hundred thousand, so he's getting back at me by asking for even more." He stared at Melissa, who sat hunched over her phone, her back to him. "He won't get away with this. Kidnapping is a felony. He'll go to prison for a long time."

Melissa only hunched her shoulders more. Erik didn't bother pointing out that the embezzlement Carl Westover was already accused of was also a felony, but the penalty for kidnapping and extortion would add considerably to his sentence. From what Erik knew of Carl, he had a sharp mind. He would know what he was risking by taking Dawn. Which meant Melissa was right—Carl was desperate. Whether he was desperate enough to hurt a niece he supposedly loved remained to be seen.

Someone knocked on the door and Travis opened it to Deputy Jamie Douglas. She glanced at the Sheffields, then asked to speak to the sheriff alone. Travis stepped out and closed the door.

Brandon sat at the opposite end of the table and buried his head in his hands. He looked totally drained, his skin pasty and sagging, eyes hollowed. Melissa, mascara smeared and lipstick faded, continued to stare at her phone. Erik wondered if she was even aware of anyone else in the room.

The door opened and the sheriff returned. Erik and Brandon looked up. "Someone has reported a car off the highway up on Dixon Pass," he said. "It matches the description of Carl Westover's current lease vehicle, the Lexus LS."

"What do you mean, off the highway?" Brandon asked. "Is it parked? Is anyone in it?"

Travis glanced at Erik, then away. "The car is in the canyon below the roadway. Search and Rescue are on their way now."

SHERI HAD BEEN thinking of drawing a hot bath and pouring a large glass of wine when the call came for volunteers to respond to a report of a vehicle off the side of Dixon Pass. She could have opted out, using the excuse that she was too tired from competing in the ice festival earlier that day, but a car in the canyon meant rescuers would have to climb down to reach any survivors, sometimes a long way, and sometimes in very rugged terrain. Everyone on Search and Rescue trained for the work, but only a handful of members, including Sheri, could handle the difficult stuff easily. And how many of that group would already be celebrating at the after-party for the festival, their blood alcohol high enough that they would have to excuse themselves from this call?

She changed into insulated winter gear, donned her bright blue Search and Rescue parka and texted Tony that she was on her way.

She spotted the flashing lights of emergency vehicles as she crested the top of the pass, red and blue strobes lighting up the snowbanks of the left side of the road in the growing darkness. She parked at the end of a row of cars on the right shoulder and climbed out, the cold that had descended with nightfall hitting her like a slap and making her draw her parka more tightly around her.

She walked up the road to where Tony and Lieutenant Carrie Andrews conferred. Several other volunteers—Danny Irwin, Eldon Ramsey, Ted Carruthers, and Austen Morrissey—stood nearby. Tony looked up at Sheri's approach and motioned for the others to join them. "A passing motorist noticed the tracks over the edge about half an hour ago," Tony said. "He stopped to take a look and saw the top of the car in the creek at the bottom of the canyon. He had to drive to the top of the pass to get a signal and call for help."

"It's in the creek?" Ted made a face. The water would be ice cold this time of year. Anyone landing in it, whether someone thrown from the vehicle or a rescuer who had to wade through the water to get to anyone in the car, would be risking hypothermia.

"I took a look and the vehicle is lying on its side in the water," Tony said. "From what I remember, the creek at that point is less than a foot deep. There's a crust of ice the vehicle broke through, but the water is running fast enough in that narrow section that the creek hasn't frozen solid."

"It's a fairly gentle slope down into the canyon," Carrie said. "Lots of loose rock, so running some ropes down will make climbing up and down a lot easier. The trickiest part will be getting a litter up."

"Do we know who's in the car?" Danny asked. "How many? What ages?"

Tony shook his head. "I didn't see anyone moving around when I looked," he said.

Not something they wanted to hear—no one calling for help or trying to get out of the car could mean the driver and any passengers were either dead, or so seriously injured that they were unconscious.

"Sheri, you and Danny go down first," Tony said. "Assess the situation and let us know what you need."

"Ted and I will handle the ropes up top," Carrie said.

As they gathered the gear they would need to descend, a new set of flashing lights moved toward them on the highway. A black-and-white Rayford County Sheriff's Department SUV pulled in alongside them and Sheriff Walker leaned out the driver's side window. "What have you got?"

"A vehicle in the creek down there." Tony nodded toward the canyon. "We don't know anything else."

"Someone called in the license plate and it matches a vehicle we're looking for," Travis said.

"Oh?" Tony asked. "Who's that? Should we be worried?"

"You should be careful," Travis said. "If the plate number is right, it could belong to a kidnapper."

"Carl Westover?" Sheri had been listening to the conversation. Now she turned and faced the others. "That's his car down there?"

"We think so." The answer came not from the sheriff but from Erik, who had stepped out of the sheriff's SUV on the passenger side. "He may have Dawn Sheffield with him."

"We'll know more in a few minutes," Tony said. He turned back to help Austen with the ropes.

Five minutes later, they had everything set up for the descent into the canyon. "Are you ready?" Carrie asked, looking at Danny and Sheri.

"Ready." She checked her safety lines, clipped in and started her descent. As Carrie had said, this wasn't a particularly challenging or frightening climb, though the loose rock did make some spots tricky.

Ten minutes later, she was standing in the ice on the bank of the creek, studying the wrecked vehicle in front of her. The stillness and silence of the area struck her—not a good sign. She scanned the area around the wreckage, but saw no sign that anyone had been thrown from the vehicle as it tumbled from the roadway above.

"A Lexus." Danny came up beside her and gave a low whistle. "Sweet ride."

"Let's hope the fancy ride came with fancy safety features," Sheri said. She braced herself, then waded into the water.

Her boots kept her dry for the first few steps, then icy fingers of water seeped in, down her ankles, and wrapped around her toes. The water was so cold it hurt, and she gritted her teeth against the pain. Only a few more minutes. All she had to do was reach up and open the passenger door.

Danny followed and hoisted himself up onto the vehicle. Working together, the two of them succeeded in wrenching open the door, which had been badly dented on the trip down into the canyon. Danny leaned in, legs dangling, and emerged soon after. "There's nobody in there," he said.

"They must have been thrown." Sheri jogged to the bank and hauled herself out again, then jogged down the bank, scanning the area. "Carl!" she shouted. "Dawn!"

Danny caught up with her, a hand on her shoulder. "There's nobody here," he said.

"How do you know?"

"The seat belts are all unfastened. The windshield and side windows are cracked and crazed, but none of them are busted out."

"Did they manage to get out on their own?" She looked around. "Where did they go?"

"The only footprints I saw were our own." He shook his head. "I don't think anyone was in that car when it went over."

"What have you found?"

They both turned to see Erik striding toward him. "What are you doing down here?" she asked. He was wearing a helmet and climbing harness, which looked out of place with his street clothes, though at least he was wearing good boots.

"I'm investigating a possible crime scene and hoping to apprehend a criminal suspect." He looked around. "Are Carl and Dawn in there?"

"No one's in there," Danny said. "I don't think they were—at least not when the car went over."

"We have to look," Sheri said. "We have to make sure." She cupped her hands to her mouth and shouted, "Dawn! Dawn Sheffield!"

She walked away from the others, and took out a flashlight, widened its beam and played it over the ground on both sides of the creek. No footprints but hers and Danny's. Nothing that would have been made by a little girl.

While she searched, Erik and Danny returned to the vehicle. Erik climbed up as Danny had done, and looked inside. By the time he and Danny returned to the bank, Sheri had rejoined them. "The keys are in the ignition," Erik said. "I don't see any luggage or clothing or other personal items. The glove box is empty."

"He took everything out before he sent the vehicle over the edge," Danny said.

"Why are you so sure of that?" Erik asked.

Danny looked back up the slope. "It's an odd place to go off the road. The highway is wider here than a lot of other places, there's no sharp curve, no blind spot, no steep grade and no shadowed area that would collect ice. No avalanche chute."

"I don't remember a vehicle going off at this spot before," Sheri said.

"The shoulder is just wide enough here to safely exit the vehicle without being in traffic," Danny said. "The slope down to the creek starts out gradual, then gets steeper. Get the car started rolling toward the edge and gravity would do the rest."

"Why do something like that?" Sheri asked.

"The Amber Alert includes a description of Carl's car," Erik said. "He would want to get rid of it as soon as possible. It's only bad luck someone spotted the tracks on the side of the road and got curious. Otherwise, it could have been months before the car was found."

"So he ditched his car," Sheri said. "Then what? He's got a little girl and maybe some luggage. We're eight miles from town."

"Someone might have picked them up," Danny said. "Someone who hasn't seen the news and doesn't get alerts on their phone. A man and his little girl look harmless enough."

"We'll put out a bulletin," Erik said. He looked back at the vehicle. "And we'll arrange for a wrecker to haul the vehicle out of the creek."

"We'd better head up top and get into dry shoes," Danny said. "Sheri, you go first. Erik can follow and I'll be cleanup man."

They made the trek up top. Carrie met Sheri at the end of the rope. "There's no one there," Sheri said. "We think the car was dumped and the driver and passenger hitched a ride from a passing motorist."

"The plate number and description match the car leased to Carl Westover," Erik said when he emerged at road level a few moments later. He removed the helmet and stripped off the harness and handed them to Austen. "He knew every law enforcement agency in the state was looking for him and his car, so he got rid of it."

"You won't be needing us anymore," Tony said.

Sheri started to follow Danny toward their cars, but Erik touched her elbow. "Hang on a sec," he said.

She sent him a questioning look, but said nothing, waiting.

"Do you mind if I stop by later?" he asked. "Just to get your feedback on all this." He gestured to take in the scene.

She wanted to tell him no, but she was curious

to know what he found. She was invested in Dawn Sheffield's safety now, even if getting involved wasn't such a good idea. "All right. I'm in the Spruce Condos on the east side of town. 4A."

"Thanks. I won't be too late."

She probably wouldn't have time for that bath, but she might open the wine, she thought as she hiked back to her car. A little liquid courage might be just the thing for her first time alone with her ex in two years.

Chapter Four

Sheri had finished one glass of wine and was contemplating a second when Erik knocked on her door. "Come on in," she said, and led the way into the living room of her condo. "You can hang your coat in the closet there." She indicated a closet that held everything from skis to some of her climbing gear, plus winter coats.

He removed his jacket to reveal a denim-blue sweater. She recognized that sweater. She had given it to him for Christmas five years ago. A lifetime ago.

"Can I get you something?" she asked. "I'm having wine."

"That would be good. Thanks." He sank onto the sofa and rubbed one hand across his face.

"Is everything okay?" she asked as she filled two wineglasses. "You look exhausted."

"More frustrated. I'm pretty sure Carl Westover hasn't gone too far, but we haven't turned up a single sighting of him or Dawn."

"My heart goes out to her parents." Sheri handed

him one of the glasses, then settled on the opposite end of the sofa.

"I wish I had as much faith as the mother that her brother won't hurt her little girl." He sipped from his glass and nodded. "This is good wine."

"You don't really think Carl would hurt his niece, do you? When I saw them, she didn't seem afraid of him at all."

"Unfortunately, my line of work gives you a jaundiced view of people in general. And anyone who would take a child away from loving parents for the purposes of extorting money has already crossed a big moral barrier."

"What are you doing back in investigations?" she asked. "When did you leave teaching?" Erik had starting teaching at the state's law enforcement academy the year before their divorce was final. He had said the opportunity was too good to pass up.

He set the wineglass on the table beside him and angled toward her. "I thought teaching would get me away from the emotional side of law enforcement. After Claire died, I had a harder time than I expected dealing with the criminals I investigated. The last case I worked was a pedophile ring. They were making and selling videos of kids." He shook his head. "It almost broke me. I couldn't deal."

She stared at him, feeling sick. "You never told me." She leaned toward him. "We were still married then. Why didn't you tell me?"

"You were struggling so much—I couldn't add

to that. I thought I could handle it on my own." He picked up the wineglass and took a long drink. "I went to counseling for a while. It helped."

"Was this while we were still married, too?"

"After. I'd been teaching a little while then, but I was still having a hard time emotionally. Leaving fieldwork helped, but there were still days where just getting out of bed was such a struggle."

She nodded. She knew all about those days. After Claire died she had spent so many months wondering why she had to keep living when her daughter was gone.

"You say the counseling helped?" She never would have expected Erik to seek professional counseling. He was always the tough guy, able to handle whatever came along.

"It did," he said. "I've kept it up, though I don't see my therapist as often. She's the one who encouraged me to return to investigation. Carl Westover was my first assignment. Dealing with an embezzler seemed like a good way to ease back in. And then he had to kidnap a kid." He drained the rest of the wine and set the glass aside. "What about you?" he asked. "Did you try counseling?"

She shook her head. "I took up climbing."

He nodded. "Pushing yourself physically can help focus your mind. I spent a lot of time at the gym that first year after Claire died."

She hadn't known that, either. Those months she had lived at the bottom of a well of grief, unable to see anything around her. "When I'm tackling a tough climb, I can't think about anything else but my next move, and the move after that," she said. "It's like a meditation, emptying my mind of everything else."

"Everyone says you're very good," he said.

Did that mean he had been asking about her? "I discovered I have a talent, plus I've worked very hard to get better."

"And the search and rescue work? How did you get into that?"

"When I took the teaching job here two years ago Tony, the captain, saw me when I was climbing one day and asked if I'd be interested. He said they were always looking for climbers to add to the team. It sounded intriguing, so I attended a training session and I was hooked."

"What do you like about it?" he asked.

"It's physically and emotionally demanding. Intense. But you're working as a team and everyone is focused on the same goal. And you save lives. When a rescue is successful, it's such a tremendous feeling of victory."

"And the unsuccessful rescues?"

"They're hard. But again, you're not dealing with the hard stuff alone. Everyone on the team is watching out for each other."

"We should have done that after Claire died," he said. "Watched out for each other. I don't know why we didn't. Why we couldn't."

His words caught her off guard. This was a side of

Erik she had never seen—one willing to talk about the hard emotions, almost as if he had been wanting to discuss this with her. She had grown so used to the hard, closed-off man he had become at the end of their marriage that she wasn't sure how to react. "We were both hurting so badly, I guess," she said. Now she was the one who struggled for words. She had wanted him to be there for her so badly in those days after the accident—but how selfish was that, when she hadn't given him any support in his own grief?

"I know you felt guilty about what happened," he said. "You shouldn't be. That's one thing therapy drilled in to me. The feeling is natural, but it's a lie."

"I was her mother. I was supposed to look out for her. And I was right there."

"She was an active, curious four-year-old. You turned your back for half a second and she ran into the street and was struck by that car. She had never done anything like that before, so how could you have predicted it."

She nodded, her throat too constricted to speak. Everything he said was true. She had said it herself over and over. But she couldn't shake the feeling that she should have known. Claire was only four. And Sheri was her mother. A mother should know better.

He moved over and put his arm around her. She rested her head on his shoulder, surprised to feel her cheeks were wet. "Sometimes I dream about that day," she said. "But in my dreams I yank her back. The car goes by and Claire is still there, in my arms."

She pressed her face into the sweater and breathed in the familiar scent of him—salt and spice and clean skin. She had heard that the sense of smell remained when all others deserted you. When she was very old, she was sure she would still recognize Erik by the scent of him.

He held her tighter, his arms around her so reassuring. She thought he might have kissed the top of her head, but maybe she only imagined that. It was something he used to do.

"I'm sorry," he said after a moment. "I'm sorry I wasn't a better husband."

"I'm sorry I wasn't a better wife." The words were muffled, so she raised her head and wiped at her eyes with one hand. "We were both pretty awful to each other at the end."

"We'd been through something awful. Something no parents should ever have to face."

"I think about that woman sometimes. Margaret Freeble." The driver whose car had struck Claire when the little girl darted out from between two parked cars.

"What about her?"

"It must be so awful for her. I was so angry and I said some terrible things to her. But I know now the accident wasn't her fault. It was just…an accident."

"Maybe you should write to her and tell her that."

The thought had never occurred to her. She stared at him. "Seriously? I don't even know her address."

"I could probably find it out. It might make her feel better. And it might help you, too."

"Now you sound like a therapist."

"Maybe I've learned a few things."

His arm was still around her, and she was suddenly conscious of how close they were, his body warm against hers. An unsettling longing to be closer swept through her. Though they had been divorced for two years, and their relationship had been in trouble for two years before that, her body still remembered what is was like to be loved by this man.

She sat up straighter and pressed against the arm of the sofa, putting as much distance between them as possible. "What did you come here to talk to me about?" she asked.

Some dark emotion passed across his face—hurt? anger?—but he looked away, and moved over a few inches on the sofa. "I wanted to know what you saw when you first came upon Carl's car in that gulch," he said.

She frowned. "It was just a car, lying on its side. Pretty dented up. The windows were cracked but not blown out. There were no personal belongings scattered about, which should have been my first clue that no one was in the vehicle when it went down there. Usually there is stuff scattered around—papers, clothing, food wrappers—whatever is in the car gets shaken out on the way down or when any survivors get out. Danny said he looked in the glove box and it was empty too."

"Carl probably thought that would slow us down on identifying him as the driver, though he left the license tags in place. Maybe he just took everything out as a matter of course. He'd wiped the interior clean, too. We didn't find a single clear fingerprint."

"Why would he go to all that trouble?" she asked. "He must know he would be identified—by his sister, if by no one else."

"I've been studying Carl for three months now," Erik said. "He has an outsized opinion of himself. He was sure he could get away with stealing large amounts of money from his employer. When he was arrested he seemed more upset that the people he worked with had suspected him all along than that we were charging him with a crime. Even after his arrest, he was sure the charges would be dropped, or that the judge and jury would believe his story and not the evidence. Maybe that ego is operating here. He sees himself as a dangerous fugitive, on the run from the law."

"He's playing a character in a movie," she said. "He crashes his car and wipes it clean to slow down his pursuers."

"But he doesn't remove the license plates." Erik nodded. "That's the kind of overlooked detail that has tripped him up all along. He stole a lot of money from his employer, but instead of tucking it away and carrying on as usual, he immediately began spending it lavishly. Naturally, everyone wondered where he had gotten the funds for a new car, new suits and a fancy vacation. It might have taken us a little longer to pin the crime on him if he had been more careful."

"What's going to happen now that he's contacted his sister?" she asked.

"Maybe we can persuade him to come out of hiding for the money. Greed has driven him all along. Or maybe someone will spot him and Dawn and report them to law enforcement. We'll keep looking and sooner or later he'll make a mistake."

She nodded. Erik had always been dogged in pursuit of any criminal he was after. His devotion to duty had annoyed her sometimes, because it meant she didn't come first in every aspect of his life. Now that she was working search and rescue, she understood that better. When people's lives were at stake, your personal concerns had to be set aside for a while. That kind of compartmentalization enabled you to do the job. If a person thought only about her children or spouse, she would never descend into canyons or climb perilous mountains to rescue a stranger, knowing it meant risking depriving her loved ones of a partner or parent.

He stood. "Thanks for the wine. And the talk. Hashing all this out with someone else helps, I think."

She stood also, and walked him to the door. "Good luck," she said. She wanted to say more— that it was good to see him again, and that she was glad they were on better terms now. But the words stuck in her throat. Because she was afraid of saying the wrong thing? Afraid he might misinterpret her words? Both?

"Good night," he said, and then he was gone, the door closing softly behind him.

She leaned against the door and closed her eyes. Erik had been so kind and understanding tonight, so smart and perceptive—the man she had first fallen in love with.

Was she so pathetic, so starved for attention that the smallest kindness from a man had her wanting him to take her to bed?

Or was what she was feeling more nostalgia for what had been, for a life before grief and anger had stolen the part of her away that could forget herself in lovemaking? How wonderful to be that woman again, if only for a few hours.

But she wasn't that woman, and Erik wasn't that man. As much as she knew how well he could love her, she also knew how deeply they could hurt each other. Ignoring that seemed a recipe for disaster. She had a lot of training in saving other people from their mistakes, but she had a feeling rescuing herself could be much harder.

THE RENTAL ERIK HAD ended up in had two things in its favor—the price was cheap, since the owners were in the middle of remodeling, with construction confined mostly to the exterior—and the bedroom was dark and quiet, at the back of the house, which boded well for sleeping in on mornings after a late night.

His job came with a lot of late nights, so he valued anything that could help him be less sleep-deprived. He was sound asleep ten o'clock Sunday morning when the blare of his phone startled him awake. He groped on the nightstand and answered, "Hello?"

"Erik, this is Gage." The sergeant's easygoing voice sounded wide awake. "We got a call someone spotted Carl and Dawn at a motel in Junction. By the time the local cops got there, they had cleared out, but I thought you might want to go with me to talk to the woman who called it in, and anyone at the motel who might have seen them."

"Yes. Great." Erik sat up on the side of the bed and scrubbed at his face.

"I'll be by in a few minutes to pick you up," Gage said.

"Give me more than a few minutes. Twenty." He needed a shower and a shave and a large cup of strong coffee.

"See you in twenty."

Gage was waiting at the curb when Erik emerged from the house twenty minutes later, coffee mug in hand, sunglasses hiding his bloodshot eyes. Gage looked amused as Erik slid into the passenger seat of the SUV. "Late night?"

"I didn't sleep well." He had lain awake far too many hours, wondering if he should have stayed with Sheri. He didn't think he had imagined the old heat between them, and he had wanted her badly. But he hadn't wanted to screw up this new closeness by asking for too much too soon, so he had made himself leave. Then he had replayed the whole evening over and over in his head, and imagined what might have happened if he had stayed. He could have woken up beside her this morning, instead of in a cold, impersonal rental.

"The woman who called in the sighting lives behind the States Inn," Gage said. "She said she saw a man and a girl that fit the description from the Amber Alert outside one of the rooms this morning. The motel owner says the man registered as Mark Freeman and told her he and his daughter were on their way to visit his mother in Albuquerque. They checked out about nine o'clock."

"Did the clerk at the motel agree that they fit the description from the Amber Alert?" Erik asked.

"She said she didn't see the girl, but the man was about forty and had brown hair, so maybe. At least if this checks out we know he's on the move. That gives us something to go on."

Erik nodded. Sometimes you got lucky. Other times, you spent a lot of effort chasing leads that went nowhere.

Fayette Roubideaux was a full-figured peroxide blonde who managed a local discount store and grew vegetables in her backyard. "I was watering the tomatoes when I saw the man and the girl," she told Erik and Gage, after she had checked their ID and escorted them into said yard. She gestured to where a row of motel rooms were visible across a ditch, on the other side of a chain-link fence. "I noticed because the girl was crying. She wanted to go swimming and the man kept telling her the pool was closed. Which it is, because you know, it's February." She shrugged. "Kids."

"Describe them for me," Erik said.

"Well, the man was a pretty average white guy—middle-aged, kind of shaggy brown hair. He had on khaki pants and a kind of dark jacket. The little girl had long hair, about the same color of brown."

"Dark brown or light brown?" Erik asked.

"Light. Almost dishwater blond. She was wearing a pink snowsuit."

Erik showed her a picture of Dawn. "Was this the girl you saw?" he asked.

The woman frowned at the photograph. "Maybe? Only her hair was a lot lighter, and she looked younger to me. I mean, they were way over on the other side of the fence."

A picture of Carl produced even less certainty. "I didn't really pay much attention to him," she said. "He was just, you know, ordinary."

"Thank you, Ms. Roubideaux," Erik said. "We appreciate you calling this in."

"Do you think it's the people you're looking for?" she asked.

"We'll definitely follow up on it," Erik said.

They returned to Gage's SUV and drove to the motel. "I'm not convinced it's them," Gage said.

"Let's see what the motel clerk says."

The motel clerk, Darius Haskins, shook his head

when shown a photo of Carl Westover. "Freeman had less of a chin and more of a nose than this guy," he said.

"What kind of car was he driving?" Gage asked.

"A Toyota Sienna. I remember because my sister just got one."

He provided Freeman's driver's license, plate number and credit card information and Erik called it in when they were back at Gage's SUV. "It checks out," Erik said after a few minutes. "The vehicle is registered to Mark Freeman of Tecumseh, Nebraska. No wants or warrants. Forty years old, five-ten, two hundred pounds. Divorced. Parents Susan and Martin Freeman of Albuquerque."

Gage put the SUV in gear. "We had to check it out."

"We did." A great deal of investigations involved legwork like this that led nowhere, but ruling out possibilities was important, too.

"Are you hungry?" Gage asked. "I know a place that has really good Mexican food."

Erik's stomach growled. Dinner had been a very long time ago. "That sounds great." They might as well get some good out of this road trip.

SHERI SEARCHED THE crowd around the base of the canyon walls for Erik. It was almost one o'clock and she hadn't spotted him yet. She should have told him to come down here, where she would start the climb. Was he in the spectator area up top?

"Oh, don't you look adorable?" Susie jogged up, grinning. "The wings are an especially nice touch."

Sheri brushed self-consciously at the fairy wings that fluttered at her back. Many of the competition winners donned costumes for the exhibition climbs and this was hers, along with a bright pink skin suit and a short tulle tutu. She had spotted several superheroes, a skeleton and what might have been an eagle among her fellow climbers. "Thanks. Um, you remember that guy you saw me talking to yesterday? The one you asked about? Have you seen him around today?"

"Sorry, no. And he's the type of man a woman notices, right? Why? Is he supposed to be here?"

"He said he would come to watch me climb today."

"Then he'd better hurry. You're almost up."

Sure enough, the announcer called her name. Cheers and clanging cowbells greeted the announcement, and she moved to her starting point and clipped in.

She was taking a route known as Ice Dancer. It wasn't the most difficult route, but it was one of the most beautiful, with mineral deposits creating a rainbow effect in the ice. The melodic strains of Florence and the Machine filled the canyon as she ascended through panels of pink, orange and green-tinged ice. The effect to the spectators should be like a real-life fairy floating up a frozen waterfall.

Near the top the ice jutted out in an overhang that could be tricky. It was something she had climbed a dozen times, but it was still exciting enough to make the crowd ooh and aah as she worked her way over it. And then she was at the top, just as the music ended. Cheers echoed through the canyon and Sheri executed a deep curtsy that set her wings to fluttering.

And still no Erik. She shook hands and accepted hugs from friends, fans and well-wishers, all the while searching for him among the many smiling faces.

"Your guy was a no-show, huh?" Susie made a sad face. "I told you—if they're not climbers, they just don't get it. You should have come to the party and let me introduce you to those Swedish guys. They were super nice." She sighed. "Too bad Sweden is so far away."

Sheri shrugged. "No big deal. Hey, I have to go run my clinic now." The free climbing clinics were designed to introduce novices to the sport of ice climbing. They were staged in the beginner area at the other end of the canyon and were always very popular, even more so when organizers could boast an instructor who had won at this year's festival.

Sheri lugged her gear to the beginner area, stopping repeatedly to accept congratulations. As she moved, her disappointment morphed to anger. So much for thinking Erik had changed. This was just like him, to fail to show today. Sure, it was just a climbing exhibition. But it was a big deal to her. It would have meant so much to have him here.

Maybe something had come up with work. She

would understand that. But if that was the case, why hadn't he texted or called? The signal in the canyon itself was pretty much nonexistent, but up top it was great. She had checked and he hadn't tried to contact her.

Lexie and Monica were waiting for her at the beginner wall, along with a petite, curly haired older version of Lexie. "Ms. Stevens, this is my mom," Lexie said. "She decided she wants to try climbing after all."

"I'm Alice," Lexie's mom introduced herself. "I wanted to show these girls that you're never too old to try new things."

"With that attitude, you can't lose," Sheri said. She turned to greet the other nine women and girls who had signed up for the clinic. "We're going to have a great time this afternoon," she told them. "And you're going to find out you're all capable of a lot more than you ever believed possible."

As always, climbing worked its magic, the hurt and anger over Erik's failure to show pushed aside as she demonstrated equipment and technique, then helped each participant make her first climb. The joy on the women's faces as they conquered fear and uncertainty and reached the top of the beginner wall filled Sheri with pride. Everyone left with a packet of information about the climbing area, equipment providers and Picksie Chix to help them continue to pursue the sport.

All in all, Sheri decided as she lugged her gear toward the parking lot, it had been a good day. Erik was one man, and she knew better than to think she could lean on him. Better to take pride in standing on her own.

GAGE SLOWED THE SUV, then stopped to allow a line of traffic to pass as he waited to make the turn onto Eagle Mountain's main street. "Is there always this much traffic on a Sunday afternoon?" Erik asked.

Gage glanced at the dashboard clock. "The climbing festival just let out," he said. "It will clear out in a few minutes."

Dread washed over Erik in a sick wave. He swore.

"It's just a few minutes," Gage said. "What are you in such a hurry to do?"

"The climbing festival. I told Sheri I'd be there today to watch her climb."

"She'll understand about work, won't she?"

Erik shook his head and pulled out his phone.

"Right. I forgot she's your ex-wife, not your wife," Gage said. "Less likely to be forgiving. Or so I've heard."

Erik tried to think of a text that sounded apologetic enough, then shook his head and stuffed the phone back into his pocket. This would require groveling in person. "I can't believe I forgot," he said.

"Is that where you were last night?" Gage asked. "With Sheri? Not that it's any of my business."

"You're right. It's none of your business." But there was no heat behind the words.

"Tell her I dragged you out of town before you had a chance to get in touch with her," Gage said. "She knows me—she'll believe you."

Erik shook his head. "I have a history of this kind of thing." Letting her down. Not that he did so on purpose, but for so many years he hadn't been very good at reading what was really important to Sheri— and she hadn't helped him out by telling him. They were married, so he was supposed to know. Except he hadn't.

But climbing was important to her. She'd been clear about that. And he had genuinely wanted to see her doing more of something she so clearly loved. He had just…forgotten. Blame lack of sleep or a focus on the job or the fact that he was out of the habit of pleasing anyone but himself. It didn't matter. She would be upset and he would have to apologize.

Gage dropped him at his Jeep and wished him good luck, then Erik drove the few blocks to Sheri's apartment. Her car was in the lot in front of her building. With a heavy heart, he climbed the steps to her front door and rang the bell.

Sheri opened the door. Her face was flushed, her hair was tousled, and she was wearing a form-fitting pink leotard that made him forget himself for a moment. He studied the way the garment clung to her curves, then focused on her shoulders. "Are those wings?" he asked.

"It's my costume for the exhibition climb," she said. "You'd know that if you'd been there."

"Look, I'm sorry," he said. "I'm so wound up in this case, I spaced it. I—"

He didn't get any further. Sheri slammed the door in his face, and he heard the solid *Thunk!* of a dead bolt being shot home. He sighed. It was the reaction he had been expecting, but he had held out hope that this time things would be different. The two of them didn't have to keep repeating the same old patterns. Except it seemed they did.

He turned and trudged back to his car. He and Sheri had lost more than their daughter the day of Claire's accident. They could never get their child back, but he had hoped they could recover some of their old feelings for each other.

It seemed he was wrong about that, too.

Chapter Five

The sheriff formally introduced Erik to his department at Monday morning's staff meeting. Every available deputy had gathered with Erik and the sheriff at a conference room table scattered with coffee mugs and to-go cups. A whiteboard at the front of the room listed the information they had about the kidnapping case so far.

"I've requested assistance from the Colorado Bureau of Investigation on this kidnapping case and they've agreed to post Detective Lester with us for the time being," Travis said. "He's been investigating the embezzlement case against the suspected kidnapper, Carl Westover, and is familiar with him. Erik, why don't you bring us up to date on what we're dealing with."

Erik thanked the sheriff and presented a summary of the events so far, from the embezzlement charges against Carl to his fleeing town, with Erik in pursuit, to the kidnapping of his niece and the demand for a million dollars, along with him dump-

ing his car in the canyon and his refusal to accept
the ransom in cash or in person. "Carl Westover is
of above-average intelligence, but he's also over-
confident and sloppy," Erik said. "He's impulsive,
vain, greedy and immature. My feeling is he came
to Eagle Mountain to plead for more money from
his sister, but before he could do that, he spotted
his niece wandering away from her parents and hit
upon what he no doubt thought of as a brilliant plan
to get even more money, and maybe a little revenge
on the brother-in-law, who was thwarting him. He
didn't think it through."

"The numbered account had to be arranged well
ahead of time," Deputy Ronin Doyle pointed out.

"He may have already had that to stash away some
of the money he embezzled from his former employer," Erik said. "Though I'll admit, that message
to his sister was the first I had heard of such an account."

"What is Carl into that he needs so much money?"
Gage asked.

"He's got tens of thousands of dollars in legal
bills," Deputy Dwight Prentice said. "That might
panic anyone."

"That might panic an ordinary person with a well-
functioning conscience," Erik said. "That isn't Carl."

"Why did he steal the money from his employer
in the first place?" Deputy Jamie Douglas asked.
"Does he have a drug habit? A gambling problem?"

"We haven't uncovered any evidence of anything

like that," Erik said. "I think he figured out how lax the accounting safeguards were at Western Casing. He saw the opportunity to help himself to some extra cash and took it. If he had stuck to small amounts here and there, he might have gotten away with it for years. But he got greedy."

"So is greed the reason he's asking a million dollars for his niece?" Deputy Shane Ellis asked.

"I think so," Erik said. "Carl has a very grandiose view of himself. He believes he deserves to be a millionaire, so why not make it so?"

"His sister thinks he wants to stick it to her husband," Travis said.

Erik nodded. "That's probably part of it. There's no love lost between those two."

"But kidnapping his niece hurts his sister, too," Jamie said. "And they're supposed to be close."

"She seems to care a great deal about him, but I don't know if he feels as close to her," Erik said. "I don't know if he's capable of that kind of attachment."

"As far as we know, he hasn't answered his sister's text, asking to talk to him," Travis said.

"There's nothing to keep the two of them from talking when we're not around," Dwight said.

"She came to us right away with the first text," Erik said. "I think she wants our help getting her daughter back."

"What about her contention that her brother would never harm his niece?" Travis asked. "If he doesn't get the money he wants, would he hurt her, out of frustration or spite?"

"I don't know," Erik admitted. "People are unpredictable, and people in desperate situations are even more volatile. All I can say is that Carl hasn't shown any tendency to violence in the past. I'd even say he's a rather passive person. That's another reason I think this kidnapping was on impulse. He saw what he thought would be an easy opportunity and took it. He probably expected his brother-in-law to cave right away and he had planned to send Dawn back to her parents in a couple of days and be on his way."

"When was the last time you spoke to Mrs. Sheffield?" Gage asked.

"About fifteen minutes before this meeting started," Erik said. "She said she hasn't received a reply to her text. She was very upset." The memory of Melissa's distress was a heavy weight in his stomach.

"Carl's car didn't turn up anything significant," Travis said. "Some long dark hair in the back seat that might have come from Dawn, but he had wiped the whole thing pretty clean."

"We've gotten calls from people who think they've seen Carl or Dawn, or both of them," Gage said. "But none of them have panned out, including the one Erik and I checked out in Junction yesterday."

"I'm still following up on a few more of those sightings," Jamie said. "There are a lot of dark-haired little girls around, and Carl's a very ordinary-looking man."

"Our best bet is going to be finding whoever

picked them up after Carl sent his car into the canyon," Travis said. "A man and a child thumbing a ride in winter on that stretch of highway is going to stand out. I want to know what story he gave the driver, and where that person dropped them off."

"What if he didn't catch a ride?" Erik asked. "Is there anywhere he could have walked to from there?"

"Not for ten miles," Gage said. "That's all public land on both sides of the highway—all cliffs and gorges. Some mine ruins in the high country, but no roads, and any trails to them are under twelve feet of snow. The only way Carl and Dawn got out of there was if someone gave them a ride."

"Maybe he has an accomplice," Shane said.

"Maybe." Travis looked to Erik. "Has Carl worked with anyone before?"

"No. We weren't able to find any close friends and while he can be personable, he's not charismatic enough to have followers. One of the reasons he got caught embezzling the money he took is because most of his coworkers didn't like him. They were only too happy to provide evidence against him."

"Any other family?" Gage asked. "An ex-wife? Other siblings?"

"None," Erik said. "Just him and Melissa."

"Find out where she was yesterday before she came here," Travis said. "Just to cover all our bases."

"I'll find out," Erik said. "I was planning on talking to her again today anyway."

Someone knocked on the conference room door,

then the office manager, Adelaide Kinkaid, peered around the door. Midsixties, with short white hair, bifocals with red plastic rims and dangling earrings shaped like strawberries, Adelaide seemed out of place in the formality of a sheriff's department—but apparently only to Erik, as everyone else accepted her as a vital part of the team. "Angie Searle is on the phone," Adelaide said now. "She has what sounds like legitimate information about Carl Westover and Dawn Sheffield."

The sheriff and Erik both stood. "Who is Angie Searle?" Erik asked.

"She owns some cabins up by Reflection Lake," Adelaide said. "They're mostly used by fishermen."

"I thought she was closed this time of year," Travis said. He moved into the hallway, Erik close behind.

"She opens up after Christmas for ice fishermen and cross-country skiers," Adelaide said, leading the way down the hall. "When this guy and his daughter rented one of the cabins it struck her as odd. Then she saw the news this morning and thought she'd better call."

Travis turned off into his office and moved behind his desk. Erik stood in the doorway, Adelaide beside him.

Travis picked up his phone. "Hello. This is Sheriff Walker."

He listened to the person on the other end of the line for several minutes, his face betraying nothing.

Finally he said, "Thank you for contacting us. We'll be out there right away."

He replaced the receiver and looked to Erik. "About nine o'clock last night she rented a cabin to a man who introduced himself as Adam Smith, and his daughter, Dee. He paid cash for one night. She didn't think anything of it until she noticed this morning that he didn't have a car. Then she heard a news report and decided to contact us." He took his jacket from a hook by the door. "Gage can ride with me," he said. "You're welcome to follow."

Erik stayed close to the sheriff's SUV on the drive into the mountains, determined not to get lost on the winding back roads. The weather was cold but clear, and the roads were freshly plowed, but still it took thirty minutes to reach Lakeside Cabins—a sextet of small, green-painted log cabins arranged in a semi-circle across the highway from an iced-in lake. Several fishermen stood or sat on the ice, fishing.

Angie Searle was a short, round woman with the bright red hair of a twenty-year-old and the wrinkled complexion of a seventy-year-old. She met them at the door to the cabin that was marked Office, a half-smoked cigarette clenched between her bright red lips.

"Cabin Four," she said by way of greeting. "I've been watching it ever since I called and no one has made a peep. My guess is they're sleeping in. The little girl, especially, looked worn out when they checked in."

"Thanks," Travis said. "Do you have a key we could use?"

She dug in the pocket of her hoodie and pulled out an old-fashioned brass key attached to a six-inch circle of green plastic. "All the rooms have security chains, too," she said. "But nothing special. Don't do any more damage than you have to."

"Go back inside and stay there, please," Travis said, in a voice that brooked no argument.

"Anything for you, sugar," Angie said. She flicked cigarette ash on the snow beside the steps, then went back inside.

Gage snickered. "I may have to start calling you Sheriff Sugar."

"Try it and I'll rip those sergeant stripes off your uniform myself," Travis said.

Gage smirked at Erik, but kept quiet. Travis started toward the cabin. "Gage, check the back," he said. "Erik, back me up."

Erik drew his pistol from the shoulder holster beneath his jacket. "Yes, sir."

Travis knocked on the door of Cabin Four. No answer. "Mr. Smith?" he called. "Dawn?"

Still no answer. Travis inserted the key in the lock and shoved. The door opened easily, onto an empty room.

Travis moved into the cabin, Erik behind him. Both beds were unmade, and towels littered the floor of the adjacent bathroom. Travis holstered his gun and Erik did likewise. Gage joined them.

"They've been gone a while," Erik said. The room was cold—the heating had been off for several hours, he estimated.

"They probably left before Angie opened up this morning," Travis said. He pulled back the covers on the nearest bed. Gage moved over to check the dresser drawers.

They found nothing—not so much as a fast-food wrapper. "Let's check outside," Travis said.

They examined the snow around the cabin, then trailed to the road, where Erik spotted a set of child-sized footprints on the shoulder. Just two prints there in the snow. "These could belong to Dawn," he said. "They look right for an eight-year-old girl."

Gage photographed the impressions, but they found nothing else. "Did they set out on foot, or did their ride from the night before return and pick them up?" Gage asked.

"My guess is the latter." Erik stared down the highway, which was empty of traffic. "Carl isn't the rugged outdoors type."

"Fishermen get up early," Gage said. "Maybe one of them saw something."

They crossed the road, then ventured onto the ice to interview the three people fishing there. One of them, Steve Gadwell, said he was staying in Cabin Six, but had not heard or seen anyone else in any of the other cabins. The other two men had driven up earlier that morning, but didn't remember any other cars pulling into the cabins.

"Let's talk to Angie," Travis said, and led the way back to the office.

When the sheriff told Angie the occupants of Cabin Four had left, she said a string of very bad words, then lit a cigarette and settled back in her desk chair. "I guess you want me to tell you everything that happened."

Travis settled into the chair on the other side of the desk. Gage stood in the doorway and Erik leaned against a credenza a few feet from Gage. The room was small, stuffed with furniture, stacks of paper, a box of yellowing brochures, a folding cot and a small wire cage. Angie saw him eyeing the cage. "We had a skunk under Cabin Six last fall. I borrowed that cage and baited it with cat food to catch the critter before he caused too much trouble." She took a long drag on the cigarette and returned her attention to Travis.

"I was back there, watching TV, about nine last night." She pointed to a door behind her. "I've got an apartment back there. There's a bell across the driveway that goes off when anyone drives in. I've only got one cabin rented right now, to Mr. Gadwell. He's a regular, from Denver. Fishes all day and goes to bed early. I heard the driveway bell about nine, so I got up and came out here to see what was what. A man was ringing the bell by then. I yelled at him to hold his horses, and went to answer it."

"What did he look like?" Travis asked.

"Middle-aged, a little pudgy, not too tall." She shrugged. "Brown hair. Brown eyes. Ordinary. He asked if I would rent him a cabin and I said yes and told him the price. He took out a wad of cash and peeled off four twenties. I took a good look at them, but they seemed real. He signed his name as Adam Smith."

"What about the girl?" Erik asked.

"I didn't see her at first. He'd finished filling out the registration card when the door opened and the kid came in. He whipped around and said 'I told you to wait outside.' And she said something about being cold. Then he looked at me and said. 'My daughter, Dee.' I said, 'Hello, Dee,' but she didn't answer, just kind of glared." She shrugged. "I figured she was grumpy about being dragged out here in the middle of the night. Well, not the middle of the night, but nine o'clock is kind of late for a kid that age."

"Mr. Smith only paid for one night?" Travis asked.

"Yes. I asked him if he was here to fish and he said no, he was just passing through. Which was odd in itself, since this place isn't on the way to anywhere, but I figured it was just his way of telling me to mind my own business."

"Did they have luggage with them?" Travis asked.

"No, but I figured it was in their vehicle. I didn't actually see a car or truck, but how else would they get up here? This isn't a place you can easily walk to. And he didn't have a backpack or anything."

"You say you heard a bell when he arrived?" Travis asked. "The kind where it rings if a car drives over it?"

"That's right. I definitely heard the bell."

"Did you hear it again after Mr. Smith came into the office?" Travis asked.

She frowned. "I don't think so. But we were talking, and it rings loudest back in my apartment, so I know to come out here when someone arrives."

"What about this morning?" Travis asked. "Did you hear anyone this morning?"

"No. And I've been by myself all morning, so I'm sure I would have heard it."

"Can you give us a description of what they were wearing?" Travis asked.

The description matched the one Sheri had given of the man and girl she had encountered at the ice festival, which matched the description Melissa Sheffield had given of her daughter's clothing.

"Do you remember anything else about Mr. Smith or the little girl?" Erik asked.

"No. But when I heard that report on the radio I realized it could be them." She looked fierce. "Don't tell me he did anything awful to that girl in that cabin."

"We don't have any reason to believe he's harmed her," Travis said.

Erik knew that the most innocent-seeming relationships could turn out to be twisted, but nothing in Carl's history pointed to any sexual interest in children. "That's good to know," Angie said.

"We'll want you to look at a photo lineup later," Travis said. "When can you come in to the sheriff's department?"

"My help comes in at one," she said. "I can drive down then."

"We would appreciate it," Travis said. "And we'll need to look over the cabin for evidence. Don't go inside or let anyone else in until I get some officers up here to investigate."

"Got it." She stubbed out her cigarette. "Anything else?"

Travis handed her his card. "Let us know if you think of anything else. And if you happen to see the man or the girl again, call us right away, but don't engage with them."

"Right." She stood and followed them to the door. "The radio said he kidnapped that girl. Is that right?"

"We think so, yes."

"Poor thing. Wish I had known. But I try not to pay more attention to the news than I have to."

They said goodbye and returned to their vehicles. "I'll bet she didn't hear a bell this morning because Carl's ride picked them up at the road," Gage said.

"And took him where?" Erik gazed across at the icy lake, and the snowy spires rising around it. Carl Westover had lived in cities all his life. Erik hadn't even come across any indication that he had so much as attended scout camp as a kid. Erik would have expected him to immediately run to the nearest town of any size, not here where there was nothing and no one.

But there was someone helping him. If they found that person, maybe they would find Carl.

SHERI WOKE LATE Monday morning, fuzzy headed from not enough sleep, still angry at Erik, and angrier with herself for caring so much. She had hardly ever thought about him in the last year or so, so why should anything he said or did matter so much to her now? She made a cup of strong coffee and scrambled some eggs, then headed to school, sure that lesson plans and her students' own dramas would demand all her focus.

By the time the first lunch bell rang at eleven thirty, she was feeling much better. The last student had filed from her classroom and she was gathering her belongings to take her off period when Erik appeared in the doorway. He was dressed in what she thought of as his detective clothes—a dark suit, crisp white shirt and tie. The rather severe look suited him, emphasizing his elegant features. "Hello," he said. "I wondered if you'd have lunch with me."

"No thank you." She grabbed a tote bag and began stuffing random books into it, not because she needed any of them, but so that he would see that she was too busy to talk to him.

He moved into the room, and she caught the scent of his aftershave as he approached. Something expensive and French she had given to him for Christmas a few months before they divorced. Why would he be wearing that scent now? He stopped beside her and leaned over the desk, one hand planted firmly on the book she had been reaching for. "I don't want any animosity between us," he said. "I made a mistake yesterday. I admit it. Gage called with a lead on Carl Westover—a lead that turned out to be a dead end, but we still had to go to Junction to check it out. I should have called you and told you but I didn't."

"You forgot all about me." She winced at how petulant that sounded.

"All right. I forgot." He leaned closer, the sleeve of his jacket brushing her bare arm. "You haven't been a part of my life for two years. I have regrets about that, I truly do. But is it so hard to believe I would forget about an event we mentioned in passing?"

"No, but…"

"But what?"

She almost didn't say but then thought he was being honest with her, so she should be honest with him. "Climbing is important to me. I wanted you to be there."

"I hope I'll have the opportunity to see you climb again. Now, will you have lunch with me?"

"Yes." She set the tote bag of books aside and picked up her purse. "The students are allowed to leave campus for lunch, so they'll be at every restaurant within walking distance."

"There's a barbecue place just as you come into town. Is it any good?"

"Very."

"Then we'll go there."

He drove to the barbecue restaurant and they ordered sliced beef sandwiches and potato chips, then ate sitting in the front seat of his car, the engine running to keep the heat going. The windows fogged and the space felt closed in and intimate. "I remember when we used to do this all the time when you first started teaching," he said.

She smiled, remembering as well. He would surprise her at least once a week by showing up to take her to lunch. They couldn't afford anything fancy, so often they ate sandwiches he had made, and sat in the front seat of his car and talked. And sometimes made out. Once he had persuaded her to have sex in the car, the possibility of getting caught adding to the thrill of the encounter.

"Do you like teaching here?" he asked, pulling her mind back to the present, away from such dangerous memories.

"Yes. I was a little worried about moving to a smaller school district, but it's been great." She crunched a potato chip, salt making her mouth water. "It's easier to get to know my students and the rest of the faculty, and the administration encourages us to be creative with our lesson plans. If I want to teach outside one day, I can, or if I want to take them somewhere local on a field trip, or do a special project, I have the principal's support. The students are great, too. You still get troubled children, but they don't get lost in the crowd, and it's easier to reach them. There are fewer temptations for them, also."

He arranged dill pickle slices atop his sandwich. "I always thought students were lucky to have a teacher like you. Maybe I would have done better in school if I had thought anyone there cared about how I was doing."

"They probably did care, but teenagers can't always see that."

"I can't blame all my problems in school on the teachers." He wiped his hands on a napkin and scrunched it into a ball. "I wasted a lot of my time not studying, and looking for ways to get into trouble. It's a wonder I didn't end up in jail." She had heard the stories before, but liked hearing them again, fascinated by the transformation from potential juvenile delinquent to cop. In college, he had discovered an interest in true crime, which led to studying criminal justice and forensics, where he had learned there were many more jobs for law enforcement officers than for forensic scientists.

"This place isn't what I was expecting," he said. "Eagle Mountain, I mean."

"It's a small town, but it isn't backward or unsophisticated," she said. "The average person here has more years of education, a higher income, volunteers more hours and contributes more to charity. And if you're interested in any kind of recreation—skiing, climbing, running, biking, rafting, hunting and fishing, hiking, photography—this is the place to be. If you're bored here, you have no one to blame but yourself."

"So I'm coming to understand. It's been a pleasant surprise."

They ate in silence for a while. When they were almost done, she asked the question that had been at the back of her mind almost since that first day. "How long are you going to be in town?"

"I don't know. Until we find Dawn and Carl, or until their trail goes cold."

The idea that Dawn might never be found sent a chill through her. "You won't just give up looking for a child," she said, daring him to contradict her.

"Of course not."

Of course he wouldn't. But she had needed to hear him say it. She checked her watch. "I should be getting back."

"Yeah. Me, too." He started the engine and drove back to the school. Students walked across the parking lot in noisy, laughing groups.

Erik parked, got out and walked to the building with her. "I can only imagine what Melissa is going through," she said. "To have your child just disappear, and then to know someone you trusted took her and wants to trade her for money. She must be half out of her mind with worry."

"And Brandon," he said. "When I saw him, he looked really rough. I'm going to their house this afternoon to interview them."

"Of course he's worried." But a father's worry wasn't the same as a mother's worry. She had seen that with Erik. She had grieved for Claire as she might grieve for an essential part of herself, which is what her daughter had been.

They reached the door of her classroom and stopped. "It's good to see you again," he said. "To see you looking so strong."

Strong. Not *beautiful* or *healthy* or *good.* She liked the word. It spoke of overcoming weakness or a debilitating condition—exactly what she felt she had done. "Thank you."

A bell rang. "My lunch break is almost over," she said.

"I have to go, too." He touched her arm. "Are we good now? Can we be friends?"

She hesitated. She had loved Erik more than she had loved anyone except their daughter. And she had hated him with the same depth and ferocity. Could she find a balance between the two? "I'll try," she said.

"I've never known you to give less than your full effort," he said. He kissed her cheek—a move that would surely have half the students and most of the administration who heard of it talking. But the kiss felt good. Warm and familiar and a little thrilling. The start of something, though she didn't want to think further than that.

Chapter Six

A large black SUV, registered to Brandon Sheffield, sat in the driveway of the Sheffield home when Erik arrived after his lunch with Sheri. He walked past the vehicle on his way to the front door and put his hand on the hood—it was cold, so the SUV had been sitting here a little while. Though the driveway had been plowed, the walk was unshoveled, and there were no shoe prints on its surface. Erik picked his way through the packed snow and rang the bell beside the door. A computer-printed sign held in place by a thumbtack read Please Respect Our Privacy. No Media.

Erik pressed the bell a second time, the deep, sonorous gong sounding through the house. Footsteps shuffled toward the door, followed by the sound of locks turning. Brandon Sheffield, in rumpled khakis and a faded maroon sweatshirt, his hair disheveled and several days' growth of beard softening his jaw, stared out. "Have you heard something?" he asked, the words weighted with both hope and dread.

"I'm sorry, no," Erik said. "I had a few more questions for you and your wife."

"Come in." Brandon held the door open wider. "Melissa isn't here. A neighbor invited her to Junction for lunch and a movie. I told her to go, to try to take her mind off everything. We've both been a mess."

Erik followed him into the great room, which looked much the same as when he had last seen it, though someone had set the child's doll up on the mantel, and two bed pillows and a blanket were spread on the sofa. Brandon sat on the blanket and leaned forward, elbows on knees, head in his hands. "We haven't heard anything else out of Carl," he said. "And then the whole business with the car being dumped—do you think someone else is behind this and they're just using Carl as a front?"

"Why do you think that?" Erik asked.

"It just seems like Carl would need help to pull this off," Brandon said. "If he dumped the car, how is he getting around? And if he wants the money, why stop communicating with us?"

"Where were you and your wife between three and seven p.m. Saturday?" Erik asked.

Brandon raised his head to stare at Erik. "We were here."

"You're sure about that."

"Of course I'm sure. What is this about?"

"You and your wife were both here, together, the entire time Saturday afternoon and evening?" Erik asked.

"I was in my office, trying to get some work done, though I've been too distracted to accomplish much. Melissa was here, then she stuck her head in the office to let me know she was going for a walk, then planned to take a shower and try to get some sleep."

"She didn't go anywhere in the car?" Erik asked. "Maybe she changed her mind and went for a drive instead of a walk."

"My office is located at the front of the house and my desk faces the front window," he said. "I can see the driveway from there and the car never moved."

"Would you show me?"

"Why? What is this about?"

"We agree with you that Carl needed someone to drive him from the location where he ditched the car to a fishing camp in the mountains where we have established that he and Dawn spent Saturday night," Erik said.

"Melissa didn't drive him. She wouldn't. The man kidnapped our daughter!" His voice rose and he raked a hand through his hair.

"I'm ruling out as many people as I can in order to focus on the most likely accomplices," Erik said. "Let's take a look at your office."

Brandon led the way to a sparsely furnished front room, the only furniture a desk and chair, boxes lining the walls on two sides. He pointed out the front window. "See? No one could move the car without me knowing about it."

The window looked onto the front yard, the

SUV in the driveway clearly visible on the right side. "Thank you," Erik said, and walked back to the great room.

Brandon sank onto the sofa again. "Does Carl have a friend who would help him?" Erik said. "Not necessarily someone who knew about the kidnapping. Maybe he called a friend—a girlfriend, maybe—and said he was stranded after an accident and needed a ride."

"He isn't dating anyone that I know about, and I've never heard him mention a friend," Brandon said. "But it's not like I know him that well. I don't like the man. I only tolerated him for Melissa's sake."

"Would Melissa know about his friends?"

"Probably. The two of them are pretty close. I don't know why. They're nothing alike. He's greedy and manipulative—she isn't like that."

"Tell me about the time he asked for money from you, before all this."

"It was about a month ago." Brandon leaned back against the cushions and sighed. "He didn't even have the guts to ask me to my face—he got Melissa to do the begging for him, which is typical. I came home from a short business trip to Vegas and she was waiting with a good bottle of wine and a steak dinner. I should have known then something was up, but I thought she had just missed me. She waited until I was in a good mood, then started in by saying she had spoken to Carl that day and she was so worried about him. His legal bills were so much higher than he had expected. She said she thought we should help him out by advancing him some money to pay for his defense."

"What did you say?" Erik asked.

"I said no. And I tried to change the subject, but Melissa wasn't having it. She said Carl was sure he would prove he was innocent of the charges and he would pay us back. I reminded her he had never paid us back the other two times I had loaned him money—once to get out from under a loan he had taken out for a bad real estate investment, and another time to pay off a car Melissa said was going to be repossessed. I had a bad feeling about that last one—I'm pretty sure that car was a lease, too. Carl let it go back and spent the money on a vacation to Aruba or something. I told Melissa then I would never give another dime to her brother, but he must have pressured her pretty hard."

"How did she react when you refused this new loan?" Erik asked.

"She cried. Then she got angry and didn't speak to me for about three days. But I meant what I said— he doesn't get another dime from me."

"Do you agree with Melissa, that Carl is innocent?"

Brandon snorted. "No, I don't. But I'll never persuade her of that. She has a real blind spot when it comes to her brother. She believes all the lies he's told her. And she's not the only one. He can be very charming when he wants to be. But I've always seen through that charm."

"What does she say about him taking Dawn?" Erik wanted to get Brandon's perspective on his wife's attitude.

"She's horrified, of course. Confused. I am, too. I have zero respect for Carl and wouldn't trust him to water my plants while I was on vacation, but I would never in a million years think he would hurt Dawn. I still don't believe he would hurt her. That's the only thing that's keeping me sane. And I know Dawn loves her uncle, so I'm praying that is keeping her from being too afraid."

"Is Carl friends with anyone here locally?" Erik asked.

"Not that I know of. I really don't think he's spent much time here at all—just a couple of short visits when we were here. But again, I'm not close to him. He doesn't confide in me and I don't keep tabs on him. I wish I did."

Erik rose. "Thank you for your time," he said. "Let your wife know I'd like to speak to her also. Maybe she knows someone her brother is close to."

"I'll have her contact you as soon as she gets home. We both want to do whatever it takes to keep Dawn safe and get her back with us, where she belongs. If I thought giving Carl money would do it, I wouldn't hesitate to shell out a million dollars or more. Melissa thinks that would solve everything, but I don't agree."

"It can be hard when a couple aren't on the same page with these decisions," Erik said. "But my experience has been that paying off an extortionist only encourages him to try for a bigger payout the next time."

"Maybe you could mention that to Melissa when you talk to her." Brandon walked with him to the front door. "I know this kind of thing can tear couples apart and I'm determined not to let that happen."

Erik got in the car and drove to the end of the cul-de-sac, where he sat and made notes on his interview with Brandon, and admired the view of snow-covered mountains. Maybe Melissa Sheffield would have a name for him—a girlfriend or a former coworker or someone Carl might have called to help him. Someone who could give them a clue about Carl's intentions or where he might be headed next.

He reviewed his notes on the case, looking for anything he had overlooked. He had missed this aspect of law enforcement work—sifting through clues and putting the pieces of a case together to form a correct picture of the crime. Whether it was tracking down a guilty party or working to build a case against the person that would lead to a just conviction, he thrived on investigative work. While teaching had its rewards, it had felt good to dig back into real police work. After almost four years away, he had felt emotionally strong enough to handle investigations again and so far that was proving true. Some cases, especially those involving children, would always be tough, but now he was even more inspired to find justice for those young victims.

He pondered Brandon's last words to him, about intending to keep his marriage together. If he could have seen what was coming, in those early days after Claire's death, would he have worked harder to save his marriage? Would his efforts have made any difference? If they had stayed together, maybe had another child, would that have helped them to heal faster?

Or had they had to go through all the pain and misery to get to the healing they needed? Teaching had taught him lessons he wouldn't have learned any other way, and Sheri had discovered a talent for climbing and a calling to volunteer in search and rescue. He didn't know if they were better people for all they had gone through, but they were different people. They didn't hate each other anymore, which was a gift in itself, considering how bad things had been between them in the end.

It was good to have Sheri back in his life. In some ways, she knew him better than anyone. She had been his closest friend and probably still was. If nothing else came from this painful kidnapping, he would always be grateful for that.

"Ms. Stevens!" A trio of Sheri's students hailed her as she headed toward her car after school let out on Tuesday. She waited while they caught up with her.

"Congratulations on winning the ice climbing competition last weekend," a tall brunette, Ella, said.

"We heard your name on the radio," Maxine, forward on the varsity basketball team, said.

"Thank you," Sheri said. "I won in my category, not the overall competition,"

"Still, it's a big deal," the third girl, an outgoing blonde named Tressa, said. "Especially since you were competing with a lot of younger women."

Sheri suppressed a laugh. She supposed to these girls her thirty-two years must seem ancient. "I think of it as having had time to gain more experience than some of my competitors," she said. It was a diplomatic answer, though not very true, since most people who climbed competitively started the sport at a much younger age than she had.

"We just wanted to say how cool we think it is," Ella said.

The three girls hurried away and Sheri continued toward her car. She slowed as she neared the dusty blue Jeep, startled to see a woman in a long black down coat standing beside the vehicle.

The woman turned to face her, then pushed back the hood. Sheri relaxed a little and hurried forward.

"I'm sorry to bother you," Melissa Sheffield said. "Someone told me this was your car and I hoped if I waited here I could catch you."

"Of course." Despite her stylish coat and expensive haircut, Melissa looked beaten down, her eye makeup smudged, her nail polish chipped. "What did you want to see me about?"

"I wanted to talk to you about Dawn. Can we go somewhere for coffee?"

"Sure. Do you know the Bean and Bakery, on Main?"

Melissa nodded. "I think so. I can follow you there."

Sheri drove to the coffee shop and parked across the street. By the time she walked to the front door, Melissa was waiting. They ordered drinks, then found a table near the back. "I know you've been over all this before, but would you mind telling me about what you saw at the ice park on Friday?" Melissa asked when they were settled with their drinks. "I think it would help me to know how Dawn looked and acted. And how Carl looked and acted. It's so unlike him to do something like this that I'm having a hard time accepting it."

"Of course." Sheri sipped her coffee, gathering her thoughts. "I noticed Dawn first. She's such a pretty child." She didn't add that she was always drawn to girls who were the same age Claire would have been. "She actually ran into me—I think she just saw a woman's legs and mistook me for you. Of course she realized her mistake right away. She said she was looking for her mom. Then Carl came up and said he would take her to her mother if she calmed down. He picked her up and carried her off. She didn't resist."

"Did she seem afraid?" Melissa asked. "Or unhappy?"

"She was crying, but I took it as more frustration than fear or sadness. She was impatient with the man. She wanted her mother, but she wasn't afraid."

"Did he seem angry? Or threatening in any way?"

"No. I thought he was a typical parent, trying to get a child to do something she didn't really want to do. Frustrated, maybe a little impatient himself. But not angry. And when the girl went with him, she seemed to me to go willingly. She wasn't fighting him."

Melissa wrapped both hands around her coffee cup, but didn't drink. "Carl adores Dawn. He doesn't have children of his own and she's his only niece, so he spoils her terribly. And she's wild about him. I can't believe he set out to deliberately do this."

Sheri refrained from pointing out that she couldn't see how anyone could accidentally kidnap a child. And that message demanding a million dollars in ransom had certainly been no accident.

"Do you have any brothers or sisters?" Melissa asked.

"I have a brother," Sheri said.

"Then you know. Carl is only two years younger than me and we've always been close."

Sheri didn't know—she rarely spoke to her own brother, not out of any animosity, but they lived very different lives a thousand miles apart. She loved him, but she couldn't say she really knew him.

"When I heard they had found Carl's car, I was terrified," Melissa said. "I was sure there had been a horrible accident. You were there, weren't you? With Search and Rescue?"

"Yes," Sheri said.

"The sheriff's department said Carl deliberately pushed the car into that canyon, but how could that be? He must have lost control and managed to get Dawn and himself out before the car went over the edge."

"There was nothing in the car," Sheri said. "Not even paperwork in the glove box. I imagine Carl thought the car was too noticeable. The description of it was on all the bulletins the sheriff's department distributed."

"Carl loved that car," Melissa said. "He drove over to our house to show it off the day he leased it. He was so proud. Of course, Brandon made Carl feel bad, because he couldn't stop himself from telling Carl what a mistake it is to lease instead of buy. We argued about it afterward. Would it have killed my husband to allow Carl his moment in the sun?"

Sheri didn't have an answer for that. She didn't think Melissa even expected one. The woman had probably sought Sheri out as an alternative to waiting by the phone for word of her daughter. Sheri couldn't blame her for that.

"I think all the stress of being investigated for something that wasn't his fault made Carl snap and do all these things he would never ordinarily do,"

Melissa said. "I blame that Detective Lester. That man has been harassing Carl mercilessly for months now. I couldn't believe it when he showed up here in Eagle Mountain. The last thing we need is him here. He's just going to make things worse."

"My understanding is that Detective Lester is working with the local sheriff's department to find your daughter and return her safely to you."

"If everyone would just leave Carl alone, he would return Dawn on his own," Melissa said. "If Brandon would give him the money he asked for, Carl would have no reason to keep her."

Sheri stared. "If my brother kidnapped my daughter, I wouldn't be so forgiving," she said. "I would want law enforcement to do everything in their power to find her—and to punish the person who took her."

"Of course I want Dawn back," Melissa said. "But I'm sure Carl will take good care of her. She's probably having fun getting to spend time with her favorite uncle."

Sheri couldn't think how to respond to this, but she didn't have to. Melissa looked over Sheri's shoulder, then stood and gathered her coat and purse. "I have to go," she said. "Thank you for talking to me."

She hurried away. Sheri turned in time to see her slip past Erik, who hurried after her, but returned moments later, looking frustrated.

"I wanted to talk to her, but she brushed me off and drove away before I could stop her," he said as he slid into the chair Melissa had vacated. "What was she doing here with you?"

"I don't understand her," Sheri said. "She asked me to have coffee and said she wanted to talk about Dawn, but she spent most of the time defending her brother."

"Do you have time to talk about it?" he asked.

"Sure. I still have most of my coffee to finish."

"Let me get a drink and you can tell me all about your visit with Melissa."

A few minutes later he returned with a large cup and saucer and sat opposite her. "Melissa told her husband she was going to a movie and lunch with a friend," he said.

"Maybe she did," Sheri said. "She was waiting for me when school let out."

"What did she say?" he asked.

"She wanted to hear about my encounter with Carl and Dawn at the ice park on Friday," Sheri said. "And she asked about Carl's car in the canyon off Dixon Pass. She knew I was with Search and Rescue at the scene." She frowned. "Come to think of it, I wonder who told her that."

"Maybe she talked to another volunteer who mentioned you were there?" Erik shrugged.

"Maybe. She had plenty to say about you, too."

"Oh?" He lifted one eyebrow in question.

"She thinks your harassment—her word—of her brother has driven him over the edge. That and her husband's refusal to give Carl more money have led to him doing uncharacteristic things like kidnapping his niece and wrecking a car she says he loved."

"So her daughter and a car are in the same category?" Erik asked.

"I don't think she meant that, but she isn't as angry with her brother as I would be in her shoes. She says he was accused in Denver of something that wasn't his fault and she seems to think if her husband would just hand over the ransom money Carl has asked for, Carl would return Dawn and everything would be fine. She even said Dawn is probably having fun with her favorite uncle."

"Do you think Melissa could be helping her brother to extort money from Brandon?" Erik asked.

"No!" Sheri shook her head. "Granted, she has a skewed view of her brother's role in this, but she seemed genuinely worried about her daughter and wants her safely returned. Even that remark about Dawn having fun with her uncle sounded more to me like someone trying to reassure herself. And when I saw Dawn, she was begging to go back to her mother. She wants to be with her. From the first, their relationship struck me as close. I can't believe any mother would do something like that."

"You're probably right." He took a long drink of coffee. "I only asked because it looks as if someone is helping Carl. Someone gave him a ride after he pushed his car off the road—someone who isn't talking. And that same person, probably, took him to a group of fishing cabins in the mountains, where he and Dawn spent the night. They left the next morning and all indications are that someone gave them a ride then, too."

"So they're still nearby." Sheri leaned across the table toward him. "How is Dawn? Is she okay?"

"The woman who owns the cabins says she looked fine. She only saw her briefly, but nothing about the interaction between the man, who called himself Adam Smith, and the little girl, whom he called Dee, struck her as odd. I think Melissa is right when she says the two of them get along and Dawn trusts him."

"What about her theory that the stress of his predicament drove Carl to act out of character?" Sheri asked. "Does that kind of thing really happen?"

"I don't know if I agree that it's out of character. Carl has always come across to me as spoiled, vain and selfish. Also manipulative. I think he's the type who would justify almost any behavior to get what he thinks he deserves. That might include 'borrowing' his niece to use as leverage to get her rich dad to pay up. He's used to Melissa doing whatever he wants and I think it's making him angry that she can't persuade Brandon to go along with his requests."

"As much as Melissa loves her brother, I can't believe she'd be any part of this," Sheri said. "I think if Melissa could get her daughter back right now, she'd jump at the chance. What mother wouldn't?"

"You think every mother is good because you were so good." Erik's voice was quiet, but his words hit her with force. "I'm sorry I never told you that before," he added.

She looked away. She hadn't been good enough to save Claire from running into traffic. She hadn't watched her closely enough, or kept hold of her hand, or impressed on her how important it was to watch for cars.

No. She pushed the thoughts away. She wasn't going to think about those things and risk breaking down, the way she had Saturday night. She shoved back her chair. "I'd better go," she said. "I have a Search and Rescue meeting tonight."

"Thanks for telling me about Melissa. She may not like having me around, but I'm going to keep looking for Dawn, and for Carl."

"She doesn't know how lucky she is to have you on her side." She left, before she said too much. For so many years, thinking about Erik had been too painful. He had not been there for her when she needed him most. Now she saw him in a new light, more like the man she had been so attracted to from their very first meeting over a decade ago.

Maybe her problem was she didn't know how to love any other man. And falling for Erik a second time was out of the question. They had proved how unsuited they were for each other deep down. And relationships weren't like tricky climbing routes. You couldn't keep trying the same route over and over and expect to get better results.

Love was more like a dangerous rescue. You got one chance to do things right. If you failed, all you could do was mourn and try to clean up the mess.

Chapter Seven

Sheri was staring down at a stack of essays she needed to grade on Wednesday evening when she received a text from emergency dispatch that a family was missing in the mountains. The lethargy she had been fighting since late afternoon vanished in the familiar adrenaline rush of being needed for a rescue. She changed into outdoor gear, stuffed food and water into her pack and headed for Search and Rescue headquarters, where a dozen other volunteers milled about. Tony whistled to quiet the chatter and filled them in on the details.

"We've got a local couple, Chet and Sarah Cargill, thirty-eight and thirty-four, and their three children—Carter, ten, Simon, eight, and Opal, four. They headed out about ten this morning to snowshoe in the Alexander Basin area. There are some heavily used trails in that area and their car is reportedly still parked at the trailhead. They were supposed to meet up with their best friends and neighbors at six this evening for dinner, but they didn't show. They're not answering their phones and they aren't at home. The neighbors drove up to the trailhead, saw the car, looked around a little, but it was already getting dark and starting to snow harder, so they called for help."

"Do we know which trail they intended to hike?" Ted asked.

"No. Though the neighbors didn't think they'd try anything too difficult with three children."

"It's been snowing all afternoon," Austen said. "There won't be any tracks to follow."

"It could have filled in the trails," someone else said. "Maybe they got lost."

"There are three trails from that trailhead," Carrie said. "We'll caravan up to the trailhead, then set out in groups of three—one for each trail, plus a group on standby at the trailhead to coordinate and provide more assistance when the family is located."

"Why do we have to caravan?" Austen asked. "Why don't we take the Beast?"

The Beast was their nickname for the modified Jeep they used as a Search and Rescue vehicle. Though ten years old and much-battered, it was better equipped than any personal vehicle for navigating rough terrain and holding all their gear.

"The Beast is out of commission," Carrie said. "I got in to warm it up when I first got here tonight and it won't start."

"Maybe the battery's dead," someone said.

"Did you check the terminals?" someone else asked.

"We don't have time for that," Carrie said. "We

need to get going. Make sure you all have all the gear you'll need." She ran through the list of supplies they should all have in their packs, then assigned volunteers to each group.

Sheri was paired with Ted and Austen, a trainee who had only recently joined Search and Rescue. "I'll drive," Sheri volunteered, and the three headed for her Jeep. They stowed gear in the back and Ted slid into the passenger seat and Austen folded his tall frame into the back seat.

"Who takes kids that young out in this weather?" Austen asked as Sheri pulled onto the highway behind Danny Irwin's truck. "And why weren't they in school?"

"Lots of kids around here are used to being outdoors doing stuff in all kinds of weather," Ted said. "And I think the Cargills homeschool. It sounds like they let their friends know where they were going, which was the first smart step."

"Do you know the family?" Sheri asked.

"I've just seen them around, the way you do people in a small town."

Sheri nodded. Though she had only lived in Eagle Mountain two years, she knew a surprising number of people, from teaching, from her rescue work, and simply because she ran into the same faces over and over again, and eventually learned names and little things about all the people around her.

"Let's hope this group doesn't end up like that

lost skier we searched for a couple weeks ago," Austen said.

Sheri shuddered. A cross-country skier had been murdered near one of the ski huts. "That murderer has been caught," she said. "I imagine these people got lost when the heavy snow obscured the trail. Hopefully, they're staying put and waiting for help."

"Almost nobody does that," Ted said. "People are always convinced it will be quicker to walk out on their own, even if they aren't sure of the way. They think if they keep walking, eventually they'll see something familiar and everything will be okay."

"It would be hard to sit and wait, not knowing if help was on its way or not," Sheri said.

"I hope for all our sakes we find them soon," Ted said. "Kids shouldn't have to be out on a night like this."

Sheri glanced at the temperature readout on her dash—sixteen degrees Fahrenheit. Even inside the car with the heater running she felt chilled. She didn't want to think what it must be like stuck outside with no shelter.

She followed the line of cars out a county road to the ski trails, about five miles from town. A brown-and-white forest service sign noted these were the Alexander Basin trails. They were popular with hikers in the summer, but saw almost as much use from skiers and snowshoers in the winter.

"Ted, take your group down Goshawk," Tony said, indicating a trail that branched off to the left. "Carrie's group will head down Sharp Shin and Danny's group will take Red-tail Trail. Keep an eye out for any place someone might have wandered off the trail— a downed tree that caused them to divert, a missing marker on a tree, anything like that—and make note to check it out if we don't find them near the main trails."

They set out, walking several lengths apart. Sheri widened the beam of her headlamp and focused on the side of the trail, searching for broken limbs, cloth caught on a branch, a disturbance in the snow or any other sign that someone might have ventured off trail. From time to time she checked for the silver diamond-shaped markers tacked to the trees that denoted the trail. The Cargills should have been able to follow those markers even if snow had obscured the trail.

"Chet! Sarah! Carter!" Ted cupped his hands to his mouth and shouted the names of the three oldest members of the missing party, and they all strained their ears, listening for a reply. Then they moved on, stopping to call and listen every couple of hundred yards. They moved at a steady pace, but slow enough to carefully examine their surroundings. The most likely reason the Cargills hadn't returned to their car was that they were lost. At some point, they had wandered off the trail, lost sight of those silver diamonds and been unable to find their way back. Figuring out where they had left the trail was the surest way of finding them safe. Traveling with three children would have slowed them down, making them less likely to have wandered very many miles from the trailhead.

"Chet! Sarah! Carter!" Ted's voice was raspy now.

"Let Austen take over calling," Sheri said. She could do it, but men's deeper voices tended to carry further.

"I'm fine," Ted said, and trudged forward once more. Sheri frowned at his back. At sixty, Ted was the oldest active volunteer, and sensitive to anything he took as criticism of his abilities. He was in great shape for his age, but a sixty-year-old was never going to be as physically strong as a thirty-year-old with the same conditioning. That didn't mean he wasn't an asset to the group—his experience alone, with over thirty years in search and rescue, was invaluable. If only he wouldn't be so stubborn about yielding to others who were a little better equipped for certain activities.

The snow had stopped, but wind had picked up, sending the tops of spruce and fir overhead swaying and hitting them with icy force in any clearing. Austen swore and buried his chin farther into his neck gaiter. "We're all going to get frostbite," he complained.

Sheri ignored him. She was cold, too, of course. But if you were going to do this kind of work, you had to accept that you were going to spend much of the time in the cold, the dark, the wind or the wet. Your muscles were going to protest from overuse, you were going to stay up twenty-four hours straight sometimes and after a bad rescue you might not sleep well for months, or might require professional help to deal with some of the things you had seen. For the people who stuck with it, the benefits of rescue work outweighed the negatives. She didn't think that made people like her better than others, only different, and uniquely equipped for this necessary job.

Ted came to a halt and she and Austen stopped behind him. He aimed his light at the side of the trail and pointed. At first, Sheri didn't see anything. Then she recognized a splash of dull blue in the shadows. Ted bent and retrieved what turned out to be a child's mitten. A very small child. Claire had had a pair like that the winter before she died.

"That's not good," Sheri said, thinking of the four-year-old girl who might be risking frostbite. She hoped Mom had brought extra mittens or socks or anything to protect those tiny fingers.

"What were those parents thinking?" Austen asked.

She thought she had grown used to Austen's judgmental nature by now, but this question hit her wrong. "They were thinking they would enjoy a fun family outing in the healthy outdoors," she said. "They're probably more terrified now than the children."

Ted stuffed the mitten in the pocket of his parka. "Let's go," he said. "At least now we know we're headed in the right direction."

When they weren't discussing the search or calling for the Cargills, the silence of the mountains closed around them. Even their steps were muffled by the soft snow. Two saw-whet owls, with calls more like a crying child than a whining saw, sent a chill up Sheri's spine as the birds carried on a late-night conversation.

The radio crackled with messages from the other searchers—no one had found anything so far. Ted reported on the finding of the mitten and Tony ordered the others to move toward the Goshawk Trail, fanning out to take in the territory in between, where the Cargills might have wandered.

"Let's stop and get some water and something to eat," Ted said. He slipped off his pack and dug out a water bottle. "Five minutes."

Sheri drained half of one bottle, then tore the wrapper from a protein bar. The bar was almost frozen and hard to chew, but she needed the fuel after an hour of trudging mostly uphill through the snow. She leaned against a tree trunk and closed her eyes, and focused on her breath. A local woman had given a search and rescue training workshop on using meditation to stay calm and focused in a crisis and Sheri tried to use the techniques when she remembered. Deep breath in…hold for the count of eight. Exhale to the count of eight…

She opened her eyes. "I smell smoke," she said.

Austen and Ted looked at her. Austen pointed his

nose up and sniffed, like a beagle trying to catch a scent on a breeze. "I don't smell anything," he said.

"Me, neither," Ted said. "Which direction is it coming from?"

She inhaled again, but the scent was gone. "The wind's changed directions," she said. "I don't smell it anymore." She stuffed the protein bar wrapper back into her pack, then cupped her hands to her mouth. "Chet! Sarah! Carter!"

A faint call made the hair at the back of her neck stand on end. "Chet! Sarah! Carter!" she shouted, trying to make her voice even louder. Then she held her breath. The faint cry came again. "Do you hear that?" she asked.

Austen frowned. "I think it's just another saw-whet."

The cry came again. To Sheri it sounded like *Help!* "That's not an owl," she said.

"No, it isn't." Ted slid back into his pack. "Chet! Sarah! Carter!" he shouted, his voice booming.

"Help!"

"This way!" Sheri said, and started moving to the right. The others fell in behind her, Ted periodically shouting. The answer sounded louder. A woman's voice, or maybe a child's. High-pitched and full of fear and hope.

Sheri almost collided with the boy when he came barreling toward them. He had big dark eyes in a pale face, and wore a red parka and black ski suit. "Have you come to help us?" he asked, staring up at them.

"Yes, we have," Sheri said. "We're with Eagle Mountain Search and Rescue."

"Do you have a doctor with you?" he asked.

"Are you Carter?" Ted asked. "We have people who can help. Where is the rest of your family?"

"This way!" He didn't wait for a response, but turned and took off running. They stumbled after him, racing to keep up.

Sheri smelled smoke again, then spotted the fire—a small blaze almost obscured by a circle of stacked rocks. A woman, wrapped in a foil blanket, sat in front of the fire. Her husband lay sprawled beside her, covered with a second blanket. At first, Sheri didn't see the other two children, then they stuck their heads out from beneath their mother's blanket, like chicks peeking from beneath a hen. "Mom, I found help!" Carter shouted as he jogged up to the fire.

The woman looked past him to the three rescuers, their bright jackets identifying them as SAR. "Thank God!" she said, then burst into tears.

Sheri knelt beside her while Ted went to see to the man. "You're Sarah, right?" Sheri said. She slipped off her pack and dug into the bottom for more protein bars. Chocolate. "You all must be hungry," she said, and handed the bars out to Sarah and all three children, who immediately ripped into them. But Sarah merely held hers. She sniffed and managed a wobbly smile. "I've been terrified," she whispered.

"I know," Sheri said.

"Not for myself," Sarah continued. "But for Chet and the children."

"I know." Sheri looked across the fire to the man on the ground. "What happened?"

"Dad fell and broke his leg," Carter moved in to sit beside his mother. She put her arm around him.

"It's a closed fracture," Ted said. "Probably of the tibia."

"Hurts like the devil," Chet Cargill said.

"We're going to have a paramedic here soon to give you something for the pain and get you stabilized, then we'll get you all out of here," Ted said.

"What happened?" Austen asked as he dug in his pack and began removing chemical heat packs and more food and water.

"It was snowing hard and we got off the trail somehow," Sarah said. "We were trying to find our way back when Chet just went down and screamed."

"I think he stepped in a hole or something," Carter said. "I heard a snap and thought it was his snowshoe. The snowshoe was wedged under this fallen tree and Dad was just lying there, all white and moaning."

"I didn't know what to do," Sarah said. "I tried to help him, but I was only hurting him worse. But I couldn't just leave him lying there."

"It looks to me like you did an excellent job," Sheri said. "You found a sheltered place to wait, you made camp and you had emergency supplies with you."

Sarah nodded. "We had fire starters and these

emergency blankets and a little food and water. The children helped me drag Chet to this flat ground. I know we hurt him, and I think he may have passed out after a while."

"I built the fire," Carter said. "My dad taught me how. You have to dig a pit in the snow and line it with rocks to keep the wind from blowing it out. Plus, the rocks get warm and give off heat."

"You did a great job," Sheri said.

"How did you ever find us?" Sarah asked.

"I smelled the smoke from your fire," Sheri said. "Then we heard you answering our calls."

"How long have you been waiting?" Austen asked as he wrapped another blanket around Carter.

"Chet fell about one o'clock," Sarah said. "We had finished lunch and were heading back, except we were lost."

It was after ten now. The poor woman had been sitting here for nine hours. "We saw what looked like chimney smoke up on that ridge," she said. "I thought about trying to get to it, to ask whoever was there to help, but I couldn't figure out how to get there, and I couldn't leave Chet."

"You did the right thing, staying put," Ted said.

"Which direction was the smoke?" Sheri asked.

"Straight out that way." Sarah pointed to the south. "Higher in elevation than this. It stopped snowing for a while and I could see the smoke rising above the trees."

FREE BOOKS GIVEAWAY

2 FREE SUSPENSE BOOKS!

2 FREE SUSPENSEFUL ROMANCE BOOKS!

GET UP TO FOUR FREE BOOKS & TWO FREE GIFTS WORTH OVER $20!

We pay for everything!

See Details Inside

YOU pick your books –
WE pay for everything.
You get up to FOUR New Books and
TWOMystery Gifts...absolutely FREE!

Dear Reader,

I am writing to announce the launch of a huge **FREE BOOKS GIVEAWAY**... and to let you know that YOU are entitled to choose up to FOUR fantastic books that WE pay for.

Try **Harlequin® Romantic Suspense** books featuring heart-racing page-turners with unexpected plot twists and irresistible chemistry that will keep you guessing to the very end.

Try **Harlequin Intrigue® Larger-Print** books featuring action-packed stories that will keep you on the edge of your seat. Solve the crime and deliver justice at all costs.

Or TRY BOTH!

In return, we ask just one favor: Would you please participate in our brief Reader Survey? We'd love to hear from you.

This FREE BOOKS GIVEAWAY means that your introductory shipment is completely free, <u>even the shipping</u>! If you decide to continue, you can look forward to curated monthly shipments of brand-new books from your selected series, always at a discount off the cover price! <u>Plus you can cancel any time</u>. Who could pass up a deal like that?

Sincerely

Pam Powers

Pam Powers
For Harlequin Reader Service

Complete the survey below and return it today to receive up to 4 FREE BOOKS and FREE GIFTS guaranteed!

◄ DETACH AND MAIL CARD TODAY!

FREE BOOKS GIVEAWAY
Reader Survey

1
Do you prefer stories with suspenseful storylines?

◯ YES   ◯ NO

2
Do you share your favorite books with friends?

◯ YES   ◯ NO

3
Do you often choose to read instead of watching TV?

◯ YES   ◯ NO

YES! Please send me my Free Rewards, consisting of **2 Free Books from each series I select** and **Free Mystery Gifts**. I understand that I am under no obligation to buy anything, no purchase necessary see terms and conditions for details.

❏ **Harlequin® Romantic Suspense** (240/340 HDL GRNT)
❏ **Harlequin Intrigue® Larger-Print** (199/399 HDL GRNT)
❏ **Try Both** (240/340 & 199/399 HDL GRN5)

FIRST NAME

LAST NAME

ADDRESS

APT.#

CITY

STATE/PROV.

ZIP/POSTAL CODE

EMAIL ❏ Please check this box if you would like to receive newsletters and promotional emails from Harlequin Enterprises ULC and its affiliates. You can unsubscribe anytime.

Your Privacy – Your information is being collected by Harlequin Enterprises ULC, operating as Harlequin Reader Service. For a complete summary of the information we collect, how we use this information and to whom it is disclosed, please visit our privacy notice located at https://corporate.harlequin.com/privacy-notice. From time to time we may also exchange your personal information with reputable third parties. If you wish to opt out of this sharing of your personal information, please visit www.readerservice.com/consumerschoice or call 1-800-873-8635. **Notice to California Residents** – Under California law, you have specific rights to control and access your data. For more information on these rights and how to exercise them, visit https://corporate.harlequin.com/california-privacy.

HI/HRS-122-FBG22_HI/HRS-122-FBGVR

© 2022 HARLEQUIN ENTERPRISES ULC ® and ™ are trademarks owned and used by the trademark owner and/or its licensee. Printed in the U.S.A.

♦ HARLEQUIN® Reader Service — **Terms and Conditions:**

Accepting your 2 free books and 2 free gifts (gifts valued at approximately $10.00 retail) places you under no obligation to buy anything. You may keep the books and gifts and return the shipping statement marked "cancel." If you do not cancel, approximately one month later we'll send you more books from the series you have chosen, and bill you at our low, subscribers-only discount price. Harlequin® Romantic Suspense books consist of 4 books each month and cost just $5.24 each in the U.S. or $5.99 each in Canada, a savings of at least 13% off the cover price. Harlequin Intrigue® Larger-Print books consist of 6 books each month and cost just $6.24 each in the U.S. or $6.74 each in Canada, a savings of at least 14% off the cover price. It's quite a bargain! Shipping and handling is just 50¢ per book in the U.S. and $1.25 per book in Canada*. You may return any shipment at our expense and cancel at any time by calling the number below — or you may continue to receive monthly shipments at our low, subscribers-only discount price plus shipping and handling. *Terms and prices subject to change without notice. Prices do not include sales taxes which will be charged (if applicable) based on your state or country of residence. Canadian residents will be charged applicable taxes. Offer not valid in Quebec. Books received may not be as shown. All orders subject to approval. Credit or debit balances in a customer's account(s) may be offset by any other outstanding balance owed by or to the customer. Please allow 3 to 4 weeks for delivery. Offer available while quantities last. **Your Privacy** – Your information is being collected by Harlequin Enterprises ULC, operating as Harlequin Reader Service. For a complete summary of the information we collect, how we use this information and to whom it is disclosed, please visit our privacy notice located at https://corporate.harlequin.com/privacy-notice. From time to time we may also exchange your personal information with reputable third parties. If you wish to opt out of this sharing of your personal information, please visit www.readerservice.com/consumerschoice or call 1-800-873-8635. **Notice to California Residents** – Under California law, you have specific rights to control and access your data. For more information on these rights and how to exercise them, visit https://corporate.harlequin.com/california-privacy.

▲ If offer card is missing write to: Harlequin Reader Service, P.O. Box 1341, Buffalo, NY 14240-8531 or visit www.ReaderService.com ▲

BUSINESS REPLY MAIL
FIRST-CLASS MAIL   PERMIT NO. 717   BUFFALO, NY

POSTAGE WILL BE PAID BY ADDRESSEE

HARLEQUIN READER SERVICE
PO BOX 1341
BUFFALO NY 14240-8571

NO POSTAGE
NECESSARY
IF MAILED
IN THE
UNITED STATES

"Ted, do you know of any cabins up there?" Sheri asked. He had lived in the area most of his life.

"No homes," Ted says. "There's a summer camp. Some church group. But it's shut tight this time of year, only open in the summer."

Sheri stared to the south, but it was much too dark to see anything now.

"Ted! Sheri! Austen!" came a shout in the distance.

"Over here!" Ted stood and began signaling with his light. A few moments later six people marched into the clearing.

Simon, who had crawled from beneath the blanket to stand beside Carter, stared, wide-eyed. "It's like the army!" he said.

Things happened quickly then. Danny, a paramedic, assessed Chet and administered pain medication, then fit his leg in an inflatable splint. They transferred him to a litter. "We'll carry you to the trail, then tow you along, like a sled," Danny explained to an already-groggy Chet. "The trail's pretty smooth, so it should be an easier ride for you."

A volunteer put out the fire while others assisted Sarah and the children. Sarah was exhausted, so one volunteer walked with her, another boosted Simon onto his back, and Sheri carried the four-year-old, Opal. Carter insisted on walking by himself, marching along behind the litter like a little soldier.

Sheri fixed a sling for Opal to ride in, facing Sheri's body. "Put your arms around my neck and your head on my shoulder," she encouraged. "I'm going to zip you up in my parka and we'll both be warm and cozy." It was a tight fit, but she managed, and by the time they reached the trail, the little girl was asleep, her breathing deep and even.

The weight of this child in her arms was such a familiar, visceral sensation Sheri felt detached from herself, floating along the trail in a warm cloud of pheromones. She had had similar feelings in the early months after Claire's birth, during early morning feedings when she would sit in a darkened room and rock her nursing baby, both of them half-asleep and swamped with love.

They moved swiftly once they hit the trail, everyone wanting to reach warmth and safety, and medical care for the family, as soon as possible. A golden glow ahead alerted them they were near the parking area. They emerged into the flood of portable spotlights, a waiting ambulance and several sheriff's department cars.

Sheri relinquished a sleeping Opal back to her mother and others swooped in to tend to the family. Paramedics examined Sarah and her children and announced they had weathered their ordeal well, and prepared Chet for transport. Deputy Jamie Douglas offered to drive the family to the hospital and they set out in the Cargills' van. After a short meeting with Tony, the others agreed to meet up the next day at SAR headquarters and dispersed to make their way home.

"Sheri, wait up!"

She had just pulled out the keys to her Jeep when Erik jogged toward her. Her heart beat faster at the sight of him, dressed in jeans and parka, hair mussed by the wind. How many times after a long call had she wished someone was waiting for her—and here he was. "I was at the sheriff's department, working, when the call came in," he said. "I had a hunch you'd be here."

"I can't believe you came all the way up here," she said. "Especially on a night like this."

"I wanted to make sure you were okay." He searched her face. "You must be exhausted."

"I should be, but I'm too wired to settle down. It's such a rush when things turn out well."

"Do you want to come to my place and talk about it?"

"Yes." She answered without thinking, but didn't wish the word back. Sitting with him somewhere warm, talking to him—that was exactly what she wanted.

Chapter Eight

Erik drove ahead of Sheri to the Airbnb he was renting on a street of older homes three blocks from the sheriff's department. He had been half-afraid she would object to him showing up at the scene of the rescue, or that she would tell him the last thing she wanted to do tonight was spend more time with him. He no longer felt the animosity that had colored every interaction in the last months before their divorce, but he hadn't been as sure about her.

Tonight, however, she had looked at him with a softness in her expression that he hadn't seen since before Claire's death. That look had made him want things he probably shouldn't want, but he wasn't going to pass up the chance to see where this new détente between them led.

He parked in the driveway of the Victorian cottage and waited by the front steps for her to pull in behind him. "This is cute," she said, admiring what was visible of the house in the porch light.

"The owners are in the process of renovating it,

so they gave me a good deal on the rental, as long as I need it," he said. "Fortunately, all the construction at this point is outside." He led the way inside, flicking on lights as he went. The furniture was simple and classic, which suited him. "Would you like some wine?" he asked. "Or tea?"

"Tea would be great," she said. She walked around the room, studying the pictures on the wall and the books in the bookcase—none of which belonged to him.

He let her wander and went into the kitchen and put on water for tea. After a moment, she followed him into the room. "That family tonight was so amazing," she said. "You never know how these kinds of calls are going to turn out—too often it's not good. But the Cargills did everything right. They let someone know where they were going to be and when they should be back. They carried emergency supplies with them. They built a fire and stayed put, waiting for help. And those children! So calm and smart. The oldest boy told me how he built the fire. And that little girl was so precious."

He heard the nervous energy behind her words. She had always been like this when she was excited or agitated—unable to sit down and talking a mile a minute. "Are you hungry?" he asked. "I don't have much but I could make a sandwich. Or toast?"

"Do you have jam? Toast with butter and jam sounds so…comforting."

He took the bread from the cabinet. "The butter and jam are in the refrigerator."

She opened the refrigerator and located the butter and a jar of strawberry jam. "Oh my gosh!" she exclaimed, then laughed and pulled out an open box of Twinkies. "I can't believe you still eat these."

He flushed. When they were newlyweds, she had teased him about his affection for what was, to her, a snack food for children and teenagers. He took the box from her and shoved it back into the refrigerator. "Yeah, well, everyone has their guilty pleasures."

"You know you don't have to refrigerate them," she said. "They never go stale."

"I like them cold. They taste better that way."

"I'll take your word for it."

While he prepared the tea, she made toast. It was nice, working side by side like this. The way they had in the early days. How much of this closeness he felt to her right now was nostalgia and how much was attraction to the woman she had become since they'd been apart?

"Let's eat in the living room," he said when the tea was poured. "I'll light the gas fireplace."

They settled next to each other on the sofa, a tray with the tea and toast on the coffee table between them. "I never did hear exactly what happened to the family you were looking for," he said. "Were they lost?"

She nodded. "They got off the trail in the heavy

snow and then the dad broke his leg, so they were stuck."

"How did he break his leg?"

"It was a freak accident. His snowshoe caught on something, he fell over sideways and it must have twisted or something. Anyway, it broke. He must have been miserable, but his wife and kids did the best they could to make him comfortable. Fortunately, he should be fine."

"That's good. So many things can go wrong in a situation like that."

She sipped her tea and her face took on a dreamy look. "I carried the little girl, Opal, all the way back. She snuggled right against me and went to sleep. Holding her felt so familiar—almost like holding Claire again." She blinked rapidly and looked away. "I guess that's silly."

"It's not silly. I'm even a little envious."

Her eyes met his. "Do you think about her?" she asked.

"All the time. Every time I see a man with a child that age. Every time I'm driving near a school or where children are playing. I grip the steering wheel, white-knuckled, and slow down to the point I've had other drivers honk their horns and curse me out."

"I could never tell what you were feeling back then. I couldn't keep my emotions in check but you were so…shut down."

"People cope in different ways," he said. Her torrent of emotions had frightened him at times. And

they had angered him, as if she was saying she was the only one their daughter's death had hurt—the only one who experienced true grief. "For me, I think I hurt so badly I was afraid to let the grief out—afraid it would destroy me."

She placed her hand over his. "I'm sorry I didn't see that," she said. "I should have."

"It was a hard time for both of us," he said. "We both made mistakes."

She laced her fingers with his, her touch both familiar and new. She had calluses she hadn't had before, and the nails she had once kept painted were short and bare. He raised her hand closer to study it. "Your hands are different," he said. "Stronger."

"I'm stronger now," she said. "Physically, and I think emotionally too." She shifted, bringing them closer together. "You're different, too," she said. "More approachable."

"I thought you were going to say *vulnerable*."

"Would you think that was an insult?"

"Not now. But there was a time I would have."

"Did therapy change that?" she asked.

"Therapy. Maturity." He raised her hand to his lips and kissed her knuckles, not thinking about the gesture, just wanting the taste of her, the heat of her against his lips. "I lost everything that mattered to me—not just Claire, but you, too. That made me see how foolish pride and my desire to be one of those stiff-upper-lip guys who were never affected by anything had been."

"Yes," she said. "I know what you mean. When I had to start over with nothing, I realized how little was really worth holding on to. Not things or reputation or caring what other people thought of me. I had to think hard about what I really wanted."

"Tell me what you want," he said.

She turned to him. "Right now, I want you," she said, her voice low and husky.

"I never stopped wanting you," he said, and kissed her.

THAT KISS WAS like an undertow, pulling her off her feet and sweeping her away. Erik reached to drag her closer as she slid toward him, their bodies pressed together, their mouths communicating without words, the messages both familiar and brand-new. She climbed into his lap, needing to be closer still. His hands caressed her, kindling the excitement of long abstinence.

She slid her hands beneath his sweater, thrilling at the feel of his still-hard abdomen. She shoved the fabric up farther and kissed her way across his chest. He shifted beneath her, the hard ridge of his erection pressed against her crotch. In answer, she reached between them and lowered his zipper.

His hand around her wrist stilled her. "Why don't we go into the bedroom?" he asked.

She was going to protest they could stay here on the sofa—why waste time? But as she shifted posi-

tion her foot hit the coffee table, almost upending her tea mug. "That's a good idea," she said.

She slid off him and he stood, then hauled her to her feet alongside him. Instead of leading her to the bedroom, he pulled her close once more, and pressed his mouth to hers in a lingering kiss. For the second time that evening, she felt lifted out of her body, floating on a surge of warm emotion and a memory of past happiness.

But this time that was accompanied by an eagerness for the future. She and Erik had both confessed they weren't the same people they had been three years ago, when they had last made love. How would that change their approach to sex? How wonderful that they had a chance to find out.

At last he raised his head, looking as dazed as she felt. He didn't say anything, merely took her hand and tugged her out of the room.

His bedroom was dark and a little chilly. He moved around the bed, switching on lamps, then turned back the covers. "Is it too cold in here?" he asked.

"I think we'll find a way to warm up," she said, then pulled her fleece top over her head.

He quickly moved in to help her with the remaining layers—silk long underwear, fitted tank, panties and socks. When she was naked and shivering, she slid under the covers and sat, hugging her knees to her chest, to watch him undress.

He was a gorgeous man. All lean muscle and

grace. She found herself searching his body for all the things she remembered—the small scar on his abdomen from surgery to remove his appendix when he was seventeen. The mole on the left side of his upper back.

Then her eyes locked to something new—a small tattoo of a butterfly above his left hip bone. She stared. The symbol seemed so out of place. Had some girlfriend persuaded him to get it? Someone he had loved after her?

He noticed her staring, and looked down at the butterfly. "It's in memory of Claire," he said. "I had it done a few months after we split up. She was so beautiful, and with us for such a short time."

Something inside her broke at that, and the emotion that followed wasn't grief, but love. She held up her arms, and he came to her. For a long moment, they held each other, together in grief in a way they had never been in the early days after Claire's passing.

Then he began to kiss her again, sexy, coaxing caresses, his lips against her temple, her throat, the curve of her breast. Desire, more potent than ever, surged back, and she arched against him, wanting him so badly.

He lay down and pulled her down with him. She closed her eyes, ready to lose herself in him, but a nagging thought made her look at him again. "Wait," she said. "What about protection?" Her face heated, and her embarrassment embarrassed her. Maybe it was the awkwardness of having this discussion with *him*. "Do you have anything?"

"Just a minute."

He got up and went into the bathroom, and came back a few moments later with a condom in a foil packet. "When the owners of this place said it came fully furnished, they weren't kidding," he said. "I laughed when I first saw the box in the medicine cabinet, but now I'm very grateful."

He unwrapped the condom and slid it on, then she pulled him to her—on top of her. She wrapped her legs around his hips and welcomed him into her, stretched and filled and complete in a way she hadn't been for too long.

They quickly found a rhythm that, while familiar, felt new. They had to discover each other again. Their bodies had changed, and they had changed—but the delight they took in each other hadn't changed. "You are so gorgeous," he said as he stroked the side of her breast, then flicked his thumb across her erect nipple. "So perfect."

Not perfect, but right now she felt perfect for him. She cupped his buttocks and urged him deeper, appreciating the dazed joy on his face, until she fell into a trance of her own, all her focus on the tension building within her, the way his hands and mouth moving over her and his erection moving in her made her feel.

Her climax shattered her, light and heat shuddering through her, so overwhelming that when at last she came back to herself, her face was wet with tears. Then he cried out with his own release and she held him as he tensed, then relaxed. He opened his eyes and smiled down on her, then leaned down to kiss her, blotting the tears with his lips, and saying nothing, because what words could ever say what they felt?

After a while he withdrew, removed the condom and disposed of it, then lay beside her once more and pulled her close. She curled into him, her head resting in the hollow of his shoulder, breathing in the scent of him, utterly relaxed and happier than she could remember being.

She thought he had fallen asleep, then he said, "I might owe Carl Westover a debt of thanks when this is over. Though I'll never let him know."

"Does he know you're investigating him?" she asked.

"He knows. I questioned him several times when he was in custody. I have no idea if he knows I'm involved in this case, though."

She rose up on one elbow and looked at him. "Can I see your tattoo again?"

In answer, he pulled back the covers and she slid down for a closer look at the butterfly above his hip bone. Inked in purple, blue and black, it was about two inches across, with the name "Claire" worked in script along one wing. "I imagine that draws some questions from women," she said.

"I wouldn't know. You're the first woman to see it."

He must have read the question in her eyes, even if she couldn't say it. "There hasn't been anyone since you," he said. "I messed things up so badly with you, I wasn't ready to risk that again."

She lay down again, holding him tightly. She didn't want to let go of this moment, didn't want to let go of him, even while a voice in the back of her mind whispered that she would surely have to.

ERIK WOKE AT six the next morning to the unfamiliar, but not unwelcome, sensation of a woman in bed beside him. He carefully rolled over, not wanting to disturb Sheri, and watched her sleep, an eager voyeur wanting to memorize everything about her, from the way a lock of hair curled around her ear to the frown line etched between her eyes even in sleep. That line hadn't been there before and he wished he had the ability to take it away.

She opened her eyes and looked up at him. "Good morning," she said.

"Good morning." He kissed the tip of her nose and she laughed and batted him away. "I haven't even brushed my teeth." He had known she would say that. It was what she always said. The thought sent a thrill of satisfaction through him.

"What time is it?" she asked, and rolled over to look at the bedside clock.

"What time do you have to be at the school?" he asked.

"Eight. I'll need to go home and change clothes."

"We have a little time." He slid down and began kissing his way along her shoulder.

She pushed him away. "I'll be right back."

"There's an extra toothbrush in the medicine cabinet," he called after her.

She returned a few moments later, breath minty fresh, and it was his turn to freshen up before he once more slid under the sheets. He would have liked to take his time, reacquainting himself with every inch of her body, but they were both on a schedule this morning, since he had a meeting at the sheriff's department at eight thirty.

She had her own ideas about how things should progress, and soon had him on his back, helpless as she kissed her way down his body, her mouth quickly bringing him to the brink, trembling with need. He clutched her shoulder in a warning that things were progressing beyond his control and she smiled up at him, then plucked the condom he'd retrieved from the bathroom from his hand, opened the package and rolled it on with an agonizing slowness that had him clenching his muscles, holding back.

Then she slid up and impaled herself on him, stealing his breath and his ability to think as she rode him. She grasped his hand and brought it down to her center. He was a man who could take a hint, and soon had her panting with need as well. They didn't waste time after that, driving toward their climaxes that, while not simultaneous, were definitely mutually satisfying.

"Awake now?" he asked, knowing he probably sounded a little smug.

"Not for long, if we keep lying here like this."

"Just a little longer." He tightened his arm around her shoulder. He wanted to savor the feel of her, naked and warm, against him.

She fell silent, the kind of silence that had weight to it. She was thinking, and not necessarily of good things. "What is it?" he asked, dreading the answer, but still wanting to know what was going on in her head. Not asking that question enough had been one of the things that had led to them growing apart before.

"Last night, you didn't ask if I've had lovers since we divorced," she said.

"It's none of my business." It didn't matter to him. He had never seen the value in worrying about the past.

"Well, I haven't." She traced circular patterns across his chest with the tip of one finger. "I guess, like you, I wasn't ready to risk it."

This from a woman who routinely risked her life to climb cliffs or ice, or to rescue strangers. But he knew what she meant—emotional jeopardy felt far more dangerous. Broken bones could heal; a broken spirit didn't always recover.

He kissed her forehead and glanced at the clock. Almost seven already. "I'll make coffee," he said. "Then you'd better go."

He was dressed and pouring the coffee when she

joined him in the kitchen, all traces of last night's makeup removed, most of the wrinkles smoothed from last night's clothes. She had taken a quick shower, the ends of her hair wet and her skin smelling of his bath gel. He handed her a mug—cream and sugar, the way she had always taken it before. She sipped and smiled, but made no comment about his memory.

"Will you have dinner with me tonight?" he asked. "A real dinner, not just toast and tea."

"As long as I don't get a rescue call, yes. I'd like that."

"Same here. As long as Carl doesn't decide to make a move and we have to go after him."

She frowned. Thinking again. "What is it?" he asked.

She shook her head. "It's probably nothing, but last night, when we found the Cargills, Sarah said something that was a little odd."

"Oh?" he prompted.

"She said while they were waiting for someone to find them, they spotted smoke up on the ridge above them—like smoke from a chimney. She thought about trying to get up there, but she couldn't see how to do it, and she didn't want to leave her husband. Ted, one of the other volunteers, who's lived in the area for decades, said no one lives up there. There's just a summer camp, and it's closed this time of year."

"It's not that far from the fishing camp where Carl

and Dawn stayed two nights ago," he said. "It might be worth checking out."

She set aside her coffee mug. "I want to come with you."

"You have to teach."

"I can call in a sub. I do that sometimes, after a rescue like last night. The school understands."

"I'll need to talk to the sheriff. This is his jurisdiction. I'm here as an adviser."

She pressed her lips together, but didn't argue. "I'll let you know," he said. "Can I call you at school?"

"Text me," she said. "I'll answer on my break." She put a hand on his arm. "I'm not just being nosy. I really want to help Dawn."

"I know." Having her with him might be good, especially if Dawn was there. Children often responded better to women, and Sheri had always been especially good with children.

They kissed goodbye and he got ready for the day. He was tired, but more relaxed than he had been in recent memory. Good sex would do that. So would settling unfinished business, which was what last night and this morning had felt like, as if he had been waiting all this time for the next chapter in his story with Sheri. He had no idea how things would turn out. He didn't dare think that far ahead. But they were moving forward again, and that was a gift he had never expected to receive.

The sheriff's department was already abuzz with activity when he arrived. "The meeting you're here for has been canceled, Detective Lester," Adelaide informed him as he passed her desk.

"What's going on?" Erik asked. Two deputies rushed past him and out the door.

"Two women robbed a bank in Junction and are headed this way," Adelaide said. "Junction police are in pursuit and have asked for our assistance. We're setting up roadblocks on all the routes into town."

Erik continued down the hall to the sheriff's office. Travis was shrugging into his jacket when Erik stopped in the doorway. "Did Adelaide tell you what's going on?" Travis asked.

"Yes. I just need to run one thing by you before you leave."

"Walk and talk," Travis said, and led the way out of the office.

Erik walked with him toward the back lot, where Travis's SUV was parked, and relayed Sheri's story about the possible smoke from the closed summer camp. "It's probably nothing, but I'd like to check it out," he concluded.

"I don't have a problem with that, as long as you don't approach anyone who's up there. Carl knows you, so even a glimpse of you might set him off, or cause him to flee."

"I won't approach," Erik promised. "I'll let you know if it's worth sending a team up there for a closer look. And I'm thinking about taking Sheri with me. If we do find the little girl, she would be good to have along."

The sheriff considered this a moment, then nodded. "All right."

He left and Erik returned to his Jeep to text Sheri. We're on. When are you free?

By the time he was back at his rental, he had her answer. My substitute comes in at noon. I can meet you then.

My place, as soon after noon as you can be there.

He hit Send and leaned back against the counter. He didn't know if anything would come of this trip into the mountains, but it felt good to be taking some kind of action. It felt even better to be doing it with Sheri by his side.

Chapter Nine

As Erik steered his Jeep up the winding mountain road, Sheri had a flashback to another trip they had made together. A year into their marriage, they had spent a weekend away at a cabin outside Estes Park. They had been like two kids running away from home, giddy with the chance to escape the pressures of jobs and everyday responsibilities. They had spent three days eating decadent meals, hiking new trails, soaking in the hot tub and making love.

Claire had been conceived on that trip, which only added to Sheri's fond memories of that place. Looking back, she could hardly believe she had ever been such a carefree, joyful person, blissfully unaware of the pain the future would bring.

"Do you remember that trip we took to that cabin outside of Estes Park?" Erik asked.

The question didn't even surprise her—for so many years he had done this, mentioning something that had popped into her head. "I was just thinking about that," she said.

"We should have done that more," he said. "Taken time off to get away."

"Would it have made a difference?"

"I don't know. Maybe."

They fell silent again, probably both thinking of all the mistakes they had made that could never be undone. Sheri didn't feel guilty, merely sad that things hadn't worked out differently.

"How far to the turnoff?" Erik interrupted her thoughts.

She checked the directions from Ted that she had written down. "You'll turn left on Forest Service Road 261A, twelve miles after your turn onto County Road 302."

He glanced at the odometer. "Another couple of miles, then."

She had called Ted this morning to get the directions, saying only that she and Erik wanted to take a drive up there. "Are you and that cop an item?" he'd asked.

"An item?" The old-fashioned term made her grimace. It made her think of gossip, or a notice in the paper.

"I saw the two of you last night," Ted said. "I thought there might be something between you."

There was a lot between her and Erik, but she couldn't begin to define what, exactly. "A lady never kisses and tells," she said.

Ted laughed. "Be careful up there," he said. "The road in probably isn't plowed."

Erik slowed for the turn onto the forest road. The narrow track had been plowed at some point, though not recently, and he shifted into four-wheel drive and steered carefully in the tracks made by other travelers. "It looks like this road gets a fair amount of traffic," he said.

"Ted told me people come up here to ski or run snowmobiles," she said. "The camp is five miles in. There's a sign for King's Kids."

Moments later, a rustic wooden sign jutting from a snowbank announced "King's Kids Youth Camp, next left."

Erik turned at the next left and came to a stop in front of a six-foot wall of snow. "I guess Ted was right when he said the road in wasn't plowed," she said.

He shut off the engine and unfastened his seat belt. "You wait here and I'll walk up and check things out."

"Oh, I'm going with you." She unclipped her own belt and pushed open her door. "The first rule of wilderness survival is 'don't separate.'"

"Sitting in a warm car is not exactly wilderness survival," he said. "I'll even leave you the keys."

"I'm coming with you." She pulled her pack from the back seat and shrugged into it.

He shook his head, but didn't argue, merely looked around, then led the way to a slight break in the snow, past where the plow had shoved most of the buildup from the road. He scrambled over a low wall of frozen slush and turned to give her a hand, but she was already over. Together they made their way through the trees, staying parallel to the main drive into the camp, which was covered in two feet of unpacked snow. Even in the trees, where the snow was less deep, walking was a slog, continually breaking through the icy crust and sinking knee-deep in drifts. "One thing for sure," she said. "If anyone else came this way, we'd be able to see it."

"Depends on when they were here," he said. "That snow yesterday laid down a good five or six inches."

"It annoys me that you are right so much of the time," she said.

"I've made my share of mistakes." The look he sent her made her shiver—but not in a bad way.

The drive made a sweeping left turn and the first building appeared—a large structure of logs painted the muted green she associated with the forest service and summer camps everywhere. She stopped and sniffed the air. "I don't smell any smoke."

"I don't see any signs of movement, or any footprints in the snow. Let's keep to the cover of the trees and get closer."

Carefully, they picked their way past what she assumed was the lodge or office, toward a cluster of smaller cabins. Still no smoke and no footprints. Erik stopped and pulled the hood of his parka over his head, and a neck gaiter over his mouth. With his sunglasses, this all but obscured his face. "Just in case Carl is here, I don't want him to get a good look at me," he said. "If he says anything, we're two hikers out exploring."

She followed his example and pulled up her hood and gaiter as well. He set out across the clearing and she followed, heart pounding. There probably wasn't anyone here to see them, but she couldn't shake the idea that a kidnapper might be watching them, not pleased to see them.

They approached the first cabin, a structure about ten feet square, the windows covered with padlocked wooden shutters, another padlock on the front door. Snow was piled to the top of the porch railings and obscured the steps. They circled the cabin, but all looked undisturbed.

There were ten cabins in total, identical right down to the snow piled on the front porches. "Sarah Cargill must have been mistaken about the smoke," Sheri said as they headed around the side of the last cabin. "I'm sorry I dragged you out here for nothing."

Erik stopped so abruptly she collided with him. "Someone has been here," he said, his voice low. He reached into his parka and drew out a pistol.

She stared at the weapon, then wrenched her gaze to the cabin. It looked like all the others. "What are you seeing that I don't?" she asked.

"Look at the snow beneath that back window," he said. "Someone has tried to make it look like the rest of the area, but it's too neat and even, and there are marks, like from a pine bough. And the lock is cut. Whoever did it fit the pieces back together, but they don't quite meet."

He was right. The padlock on the shutters hung crooked, the hasp in two pieces.

Erik made a wide berth around the window, pausing halfway to fish something out of the snow. He held up a pair of bolt cutters. "I'm betting these came from somewhere on the property," he said. "A toolshed or something." He set the cutters to one side, then came to stand under the window, very close to the cabin. He stared up at the lock, then reached up with gloved hands and carefully unhooked it. "I'm going to look inside," he said.

He pocketed the lock, then folded back the shutters. The window sash rose easily, and within seconds he had heaved himself over the sill.

Sheri didn't wait, but followed him. He scowled, but only said, "Don't touch anything."

Whoever had been here hadn't tried to hide their presence. Dirty dishes were piled on the table and a trash can in the corner overflowed with wrappers. Downstairs one of two double beds was unmade, sheets trailing to the floor. Ashes filled the fireplace. Erik leaned down and held his hand over the hearth. "Cold," he said.

"The room is cold, too," she said. "I think whoever was here has been gone a while."

"I'm going to look upstairs." He motioned toward a ladder that led to a loft. She waited until he was up there before she followed. She emerged onto a wooden platform furnished with a row of twin beds. The end bed showed signs of having been slept in, the indentation of a small body on the pillow and mattress.

Sheri stared at that child-sized imprint. "They were here," she said. "Carl slept downstairs, and Dawn slept up here."

"We don't know it was them," he said. "Wasn't there some serial murderer hiding out in this area a couple of weeks ago?"

"He was traveling alone, and he was captured more than two weeks ago," she said. "This looks more recent." She bent and laid a hand on the bed.

"Please don't touch anything," Erik said.

She pulled back her hand and straightened, then a scrap of blue paper caught her eye, wedged between two logs, just to the left of the headboard. "Erik, look at this."

He joined her, then reached out and plucked the paper from where it was wedged. Still wearing gloves, he opened it and laid it on the blanket. They bent, heads together, and read the neatly printed note: *To whoever finds this. My uncle says we are going to Mexico. I don't want to go and...* The note ended abruptly, as if whoever had been writing it had been interrupted.

Sheri was still staring at the note when she felt Erik's gaze on her. She turned her head and their eyes met. "I'm sure Dawn wrote this," she said.

"What makes you so sure?"

"It mentions her uncle. That has to be Carl."

He took a clear envelope from the pocket of his parka, unfolded it and held it open. "Slide it in here," he said. "But carefully. Handle it by the edges."

She did as he asked and he labeled the envelope with the date, time and location, then had her sign her name. Then he slipped the envelope into his inside coat pocket. "What made you look there?" he asked.

"Do you remember how Claire used to hide things around her room?"

"Like a squirrel." He swallowed, the play of strong emotion so clear on his face. She took his hand and squeezed it, then turned away.

"We should tell someone," she said. "Maybe they can be tracked."

They exited the cabin the way they had come in. Erik closed the shutters over the window and rehung the padlock. Then they retraced their steps back to the road leading into the camp.

"They must have left yesterday," Erik said as they trudged along. "After Mrs. Cargill saw the smoke, but before the snow stopped."

"I don't think the snow stopped until early this morning," Sheri said.

"That gives them a lot of hours. And they didn't walk out of here. Well, they may have walked out of the camp, but someone must have picked them up on the road."

"The same person who gave them a ride before?" she asked.

"Either that, or Carl has a whole network of friends we don't know about."

They reached the wall of snow that blocked the drive and made their way around it. They were almost to the car once more when Erik stopped again and swore. Sheri followed his gaze and her heart sank. "The tires!" All four tires on the Jeep were flat, the rims sinking into the snow. She looked around them, but saw no one.

"Who did this?" she asked.

"It could be Carl," Erik said. He moved closer to the Jeep and stared down at clear footprints in the snow. "He knows me. If he spotted me before I put my jacket hood up, he probably recognized me."

"But we thought he was long gone." Her stomach lurched at the thought of a criminal deliberately stranding them.

"I think he's probably gone now." Erik moved to study a fresh set of tire tracks that had pulled over just behind his Jeep. "Studded snow tires," he said. "They could have swung in here to pick up Carl and Dawn." He pointed to two sets of footprints—one large and one small. "They were probably waiting somewhere close when we showed up. Carl punctured my tires to make sure I couldn't follow too close." He pulled out his cell phone. "No signal. No surprise there. Carl probably knew that, too."

"What are we going to do?" Sheri hugged her arms around her middle. Already, she felt colder.

She had been looking forward to returning to the warm car.

"The sheriff knows where I was headed," he said. "And you told your friend Ted. When we don't show up in a few hours, someone will raise the alarm and come looking for us."

A few hours was a long time to wait in the cold, even in the Jeep with the heater running. She groaned.

Erik took out a small notebook. "I'll leave a note on the Jeep and we'll go back to the camp," he said. "We'll try to break into one of the other cabins. I'd just as soon not disturb the cabin Carl was in."

"I guess if you're a cop, it's okay," she said.

"My being a cop doesn't make it okay," he said. "But this being an emergency does. I'll pay for a new lock and we'll clean up after ourselves." He finished writing his note and left it under the windshield wiper, then turned to her. "Let's go. We might as well try to make ourselves comfortable."

ERIK CHOSE THE cabin closest to the main lodge for their refuge. "It will be easier for the sheriff's deputies to find us here," he explained.

"But how are we going to get in?" Sheri eyed the padlock on the door.

"The same way whoever broke into the other cabin got in. With those bolt cutters."

"I'm coming with you to get them," Sheri said.

"I won't argue with that," Erik said. "I don't intend to let you out of my sight as long as there's a chance Carl—or whoever ruined my tires—is still around."

She paled. "You don't think he's still here, do you?"

"I don't think so, but we won't take any chances." He gave her a brief hug, then they set out for the other cabin. He retrieved the bolt cutters, keeping his gloves on and grasping them high on the handles, well above where someone would usually hold them. Back at the cabin he severed the lock and pushed open the door.

"This doesn't look too bad," Sheri said. She stood in the middle of the room and turned a slow circle. Unlike the cabin the intruder had stayed in, this one was furnished with four sets of bunk beds, arranged on three walls, with a dusty iron woodstove on the fourth wall, and a large wooden table and chairs in the center of the room. "Spartan, but in good shape."

"I saw a bunch of firewood by the lodge," he said. "Let's get some."

Together, they carried armloads of wood and dumped them in the wood box by the stove, then removed their gloves, hats and parkas. He started a fire while she searched the single closet in one corner of the room. This yielded a pile of blankets, a Scrabble game, a teakettle, a stack of plastic cups and a half-empty jar of instant coffee. She filled the kettle from a water bottle in her pack and set it on top of the stove, then laid out beef jerky, two candy bars and two packets of hot cocoa mix. "You can have coffee, hot chocolate or mix them for mocha," she said.

"A hot drink sounds good," he said. "Though it may be a while before this fire is hot enough to boil water." He rose from in front of the stove and joined her at the table. "So much for our dinner date."

"I'll take a rain check," she said. She surveyed the items on the table in front of them. "I suppose we could play Scrabble while we wait."

"I have a better idea." He pulled her close and kissed her. She relaxed against him, and wrapped her arms around his neck.

"I like the way you think," she said, smiling up at him.

He kissed her again, then looked around for someplace more comfortable. They could spread the blankets on one of the bunks, though it wasn't the most romantic setup. "This isn't exactly like the cabin in Estes Park," he said.

"No, this is like the place we stayed on that lake in Idaho," she said. "The one where we had booked this deluxe cabin and ended up in an old toolshed or something."

He laughed. "Oh, I remember. What was their story—that the cabin we were supposed to have had burned down the week before and they were booked up?"

She nodded. "Something like that. Then they put us in that building they were using to store old furniture."

"Everything was mismatched and had all the romance of, well, a toolshed."

"We probably should have complained, but we were so glad just to be somewhere together that we didn't." She slid her hands beneath his sweater, her fingers warm against his skin. "We had a great time just being together."

"We did." He cradled the back of her head. "How did we lose that?"

"You know how," she said. "After we lost Claire, we could never be that innocent and carefree again."

"I think one of the worst things about those first months after she died was that I hurt so much myself— but I also hurt for you. I knew you were suffering and there was nothing I could do to fix it. I felt so empty and useless."

"You should have told me," she said.

"I didn't have the words."

She pulled his head down to hers, their foreheads touching, a moment of such tenderness he felt a tightness in the back of his throat, grief for all the time they had wasted, and gratitude that at least they had this moment.

He didn't know how long they stood like that, the fire crackling in the stove, warmth gradually filling the cabin, a deeper heat spreading through him. She reached down and lowered his zipper, and began kissing the side of his neck, stoking the fire within.

Then a pounding on the door made her yelp and

jump away. He had the presence of mind to zip his pants as Gage Walker shouted, "Erik, is that you in there?"

Chapter Ten

When Erik hadn't checked in with Travis after a couple of hours, the sheriff had been concerned enough to send Gage to look for him. Gage had spotted Erik's Jeep, and smoke from the wood stove had led him to the cabin where he and Sheri were sheltering.

A sweep of King's Kids camp turned up nothing that would prove Carl and Dawn had been there. Deputies collected some fibers and hairs and carefully preserved them, but at this point the sheriff felt they couldn't justify the expense of DNA testing, and Erik's bosses with the state agreed.

The next morning, Erik decided to question the Sheffields again, but rather than talk to them in their home, he asked them to come to the sheriff's department. "If they're hiding something, I want to make them a little uneasy," he explained to the sheriff.

"What do you think they're hiding?" Travis asked.

"I don't know," he admitted. "Maybe they've had some communication from Carl that they haven't shared with us. Maybe before he took Dawn he made a threat or said something that hinted he might do something like this and they don't want to admit they didn't take him seriously. Or maybe they have an idea who might be helping him and are protecting that person for some reason. I'd like a uniformed deputy to be in the room when I question them, as another way to impress upon them that this is a serious part of the investigation."

"Deputy Douglas," Travis said. "She looks sympathetic, but she won't stand for anything out of line."

Melissa Sheffield answered Erik's call to the couple's landline. "Do you have any news?" she asked.

"We've had one small development," Erik said. "I'd like to talk to you and your husband about it. Can you be at the sheriff's department at ten thirty?"

"Why do we have to come there?" she asked. "Why can't you come here?"

"I need you and your husband to be here. I can send a deputy to pick you up if you like."

"Absolutely not. I really don't see why we have to talk to you at all. Our daughter is missing and instead of spending your time out looking for her, you're wasting time interrogating us as if we were somehow involved. It's disgraceful."

Her voice caught and he pictured her working up to full-blown sobbing. He couldn't decide if this was real distress or an act to make him back off. It didn't matter. He wasn't going to give ground. "We are working very hard to see that Dawn is safely returned to you," he said. "You are the one person who knows more about her kidnapper than anyone. Without even realizing it, you may have the key that will help us find him and Dawn. It's very important that you help us—that you help Dawn—by coming to the sheriff's department and talking to us."

"I've told you everything I know. Answering more questions isn't going to help. You're just harassing us, the way you did my brother."

"Detective?" Brandon Sheffield's voice broke in. "What time do you need to see us?"

"Ten thirty. At the sheriff's department in Eagle Mountain."

"We'll be there," Brandon said.

"Thank you."

Brandon hung up and Erik opened his notebook to prepare for the interview. He didn't envy Sheffield the argument he would probably have with his wife. Erik didn't know what kind of person she was under normal circumstances, but stress didn't bring out the best in anyone.

At ten thirty-five Adelaide announced that the Sheffields had arrived, and Erik sent Jamie to escort them from the lobby to the interview room. He wondered if the five-minute delay in their arrival had been deliberate. Given the absence of traffic on most local roads, coupled with Melissa's objection to having to come here to speak with him, he decided it probably was.

The door to the interview room opened and Melissa swept in, head high, like a model striding down the catwalk. She wore fitted leather trousers, a leather jacket, black leather boots and a black turtleneck sweater. She looked like a glamorous cat burglar. Brandon followed, shoulders hunched, deep shadows beneath his eyes. Unlike his wife, he hadn't dressed to impress. He wore the same wrinkled khakis and flannel shirt he'd had on when Erik had visited his house on Monday.

Deputy Douglas closed the door behind her as she entered and remained standing as the Sheffields advanced toward Erik, who stood behind the gray steel table in the center of the room. "Please, have a seat," he said, indicating the two chairs across from him.

"I told Brandon we should have our lawyer with us," Melissa said.

"You may certainly do that," Erik said. "How soon can your attorney be here?"

"He's in Denver," she said. "I'm sure he would have to clear his schedule and travel here."

"Time is very important in a case like this," Erik said. "The sooner you can provide the information I need, the better our chances of finding Carl right away."

Brandon put a hand on his wife's shoulder. "Let's see what the detective needs to know," he said. He pulled out a chair and she sat in it, then he took his place beside her.

Erik consulted his notes, a touch of drama he really didn't need. "Yesterday, we received information that someone was occupying a cabin at a closed summer camp a few miles from the fishing cabins where Carl and Dawn were last seen," he said. "By the time we got to the camp, whoever had been there was gone, but we found this note." He slid the small piece of paper in its clear evidence envelope toward them. "Do you recognize this handwriting?" he asked.

Brandon leaned forward and read the note out loud. "My uncle is taking me to Mexico and I don't want to go." He looked up, eyes wide. "Do you think Dawn wrote this?"

"Do you recognize the handwriting?" Erik asked again.

Brandon looked down at the note once more. "I don't know. I think it could be Dawn's handwriting. Mel, what do you think?"

"I think it's ridiculous to think an eight-year-old has any kind of definable handwriting," Melissa said. "Anyone could have written that note. Maybe one of the campers who stay there in the summer."

Erik took the note and tucked it back into his folder. Brandon watched him, looking sadder than ever. "Has Carl ever been to Mexico?" he asked.

Brandon looked at his wife. "Mel?"

"I have no idea if Carl has been to Mexico."

"I understood the two of you are close," Erik said. "Has he ever mentioned traveling to Mexico, either for work or for a vacation?"

"I don't believe so. No."

"Maybe Dawn misunderstood," Brandon said. "Maybe he meant New Mexico."

"Why New Mexico?" Erik asked.

"Really, Brand, that's stretching things," Melissa said. "Dawn is smart enough not to confuse a state with a country."

Brandon ignored her. "Carl dated a woman from Santa Fe for a while," he said.

"When was this?" Erik asked. "What was her name?"

"Last year sometime. He brought her to a barbecue at our house in Denver." He looked to his wife once more. "Don't you remember, Mel? A very pretty woman. What was her name? Margery or Maude. Something with an *M*."

"I don't remember," Melissa said.

Erik hadn't uncovered anyone like that in his recent investigations of Carl's activities. "Are they still seeing each other?" he asked.

"I don't think so," Brandon said. "I haven't heard him talk about her in months."

"When was the last time Carl was in New Mexico?" Erik asked. "Do you know?"

"I don't," Brandon said. "Mel, has he mentioned New Mexico to you?"

"No." She folded her arms over her chest. "You're wasting your time," she said. "Why aren't you out looking for Dawn?"

"Every law enforcement officer in this state and the surrounding states are on the lookout for a man and a girl meeting Carl's and Dawn's descriptions," Erik said. "It would be much more helpful if we were able to pinpoint the most likely locations Carl would run to. Did he have a favorite vacation spot? A best friend or other relative he would turn to for help? Has he mentioned anyplace lately? Maybe he said something like 'when my trial is over, I'm going to…'"

Brandon shook his head. "If he did, I don't remember," he said.

"He didn't." Melissa turned on her husband. "Instead of trying to guess where Carl might be hiding, we should text him and tell him we have the money he wants. We can wire it to his account and I'm sure he'll return Dawn to us."

"Mel, a million dollars isn't a sum I can pull together in a matter of hours, even if I did think it would help," Brandon said. "And what's to stop Carl from taking the money and keeping Dawn? He might think he can keep squeezing us by threatening her."

"Carl wouldn't do that. Why do you have such a horrible opinion of my brother?"

"How can you not have a horrible opinion of him?" Brandon's voice rose and he stood, his chair scraping the floor as he shoved it back. "He kidnapped our daughter. Any ounce of sympathy I might have ever had for him vanished when he did that."

"Mrs. Sheffield, do you have any idea who might be helping your brother evade authorities?" Erik asked. "Someone picked him up when he dumped his car in the canyon, and that same person may have provided transportation from the fishing cabins to the summer camp and away from there, too."

"I don't know. And I'm done here." She stood also and stalked to the door, but Jamie stepped in front of it.

"Are you holding us prisoner now?" Melissa asked. "What are you charging us with?"

"Mel, calm down," Brandon said. "You're not making this any easier."

"Why should I make 'this' easy on anyone?" she asked. "Our little girl in missing. There's nothing easy about that."

"You're free to go," Erik said. "If you think of anything that might help, no matter how small, contact me at any time,"

"We will," Brandon said, and led his wife from the room.

Erik sat at the table once more. Finding a woman in Santa Fe whose first name began with *M* was going to be impossible without more information.

Jamie returned to the room. "Do you think the Sheffields were telling the truth?" he asked.

"He is. And she probably is, too," Jamie said. "But then, some people are very good liars."

"She's angry with me, and with her husband," Erik said. "She's furious with everyone but her brother, the man who kidnapped her daughter."

"Maybe admitting he's guilty is too hard for her," Jamie said. "She has this image of him built up in her mind and even though he's not living up to that image, she's not ready to let it go."

"She wants her daughter safe, but she doesn't want her brother punished."

"Something like that," Jamie said. "Family relationships can be pretty complicated."

"I love my brother, but if he stole my kid I'd punish him myself," Erik said. "I wouldn't be defending him to law enforcement officers who were trying to help me."

"But you're a cop. Not everyone sees us the same way."

True enough. He gathered his papers and stood. "Thanks for your help. And for sharing your impressions."

"What are you going to do now?"

"I'm going to go over everything we know again and hope something comes to light that I missed before. We may have no choice but to wait for Carl to make the next move."

WHEN ERIK TEXTED Sheri Thursday afternoon and suggested they have their delayed dinner that night, she fought an internal battle for five minutes. Yes, she had already agreed to have dinner with him, and part of her ached to see him again. Yet what she thought of as the more rational part of herself was alarmed by the easy way he had slipped back into her life. Could good sex (okay, great sex) now make up for the pain he had caused her in the past? He said he had changed, that therapy had helped him to see how he had failed her, but was that really true, or something he said because he wanted her back in his bed?

I'm exhausted and need to take a break tonight, she texted back.

OK.

She stared at the two-letter reply and tried to figure out what it meant. Was he really okay with not seeing her? Was that a good thing or a bad thing? He hadn't even tried to change her mind. Was he respecting her choices or did he not care as deeply as she thought?

"Arrgh!" She was as bad as one of her students, overthinking everything, analyzing every word and gesture for some clue as to where this relationship was going. Sometimes OK just meant OK. She tossed the phone to one side and turned back to the laptop, open to the student essays she really should be grading. Three. She would do three of them, then call it a night. She opened the first file. She had assigned her class to write about someone in their life whom they admired. The first girl wrote about her grandfather and, except for an unfortunate overuse of the word *great*, it was well done. The next student, a boy, wrote about his mom, who was raising him and his sister by herself since their father had died. It was touching and well-written, and earned him an A.

The last of the three was authored by another girl, who had chosen to write about her younger brother, who had battled a brain tumor, multiple surgeries and chemotherapy since the age of seven. "He has overcome so much and remained positive and strong the whole time," she wrote. "I would do anything for him, and I know he would do the same for me."

Sheri wondered what it would be like to have that kind of bond with another person. She loved her brother and enjoyed being with him, but they could go years without seeing each other. They had grown up together, but each in their own sphere of different interests and different friends. When she had married Erik, she believed she had found the one person who would always be there for her, but it hadn't worked out that way. What if the person you felt that way about wasn't a romantic partner, but a sibling?

She shut down the laptop and was contemplating which frozen meal to reheat for dinner when a text from Search and Rescue came in: South Falls slide caught two vehicles. One a school van.

South Falls was a notorious avalanche chute on Dixon Pass. The highway department regularly launched explosives to clear the chute in order to prevent exactly this kind of accident, but nature didn't always operate on a schedule. Quickly, she changed clothes and gathered her gear, her mind racing. A school van meant students were involved, probably returning from a sports activity. Had the van been swept off the road altogether, or was it trapped in snow packed like concrete around the vehicle? Was anyone injured? She prayed no one was dead.

Focus, she reminded herself. She couldn't prevent what had already happened. Her job was to show up and help in any way she could.

Chapter Eleven

The fifteen-passenger van lay on its side thirty yards below the road, wedged against a large boulder and almost completely buried in snow and debris. The second vehicle, a black Ford Expedition with a single occupant, was still on the roadway, also buried in snow. By the time Search and Rescue arrived, in the once-more-operational Beast, sheriff's deputies had closed the road and sent for equipment to clear the blockage. Sheri searched for Erik, but didn't see him in the glow of red and blue oscillating lights.

"Let's get some lines run down to the van," Carrie directed. Tony was out of town so as lieutenant, Carrie was in charge. "I want two people down there to assess the situation. Sheri, you and Hannah go."

Hannah Richards, a paramedic, shouldered a pack full of medical gear and helped Sheri stock her own pack with things they might need—cervical collars, splints and various other braces and bandages. They would assess who needed to be transported on a litter and who could walk out on their own. And if necessary, who would be brought up later, in a body bag.

While Hannah and Sheri packed, Ted and Eldon Ramsey inspected the South Falls chute. If they determined it held enough snow to run again, the rescuers would have to wait for the highway department to come out and clear it before they could do much more. The last thing anyone wanted was for accident victims to be pulled from the vehicles only to be swept away by a second slide.

"We don't think it's going to run again," Ted reported when he and Eldon returned to the group at the edge of the road. By this time one of the sheriff's deputies had shoveled enough snow away from the SUV for the driver to roll down the window and speak to them.

The woman's voice carried well in the clear night air and Sheri was startled to hear Melissa Sheffield say, "I'm all right. I'm just a little shaken. I was driving along and suddenly I couldn't see anything but white, and the car wasn't moving. It was the strangest sensation."

Sheri hurried to the SUV. "Ms. Sheffield, what are you doing out here alone?" she asked.

Melissa stared at her a long moment, then apparently recognized her. "I couldn't sit still," she said. "So I went for a drive."

"This really isn't the place to go for a casual drive at night," Ted said.

"Were you looking for Dawn?" Sheri asked. It was the kind of thing she would have done.

Some of the tension left Melissa's expression. "Yes. I thought I could find that summer camp the detective told us about—the one where he thought Dawn and Carl were staying. But everything is so confusing in the dark. I got lost and had to turn around and head home."

Sheri reached in and patted the other woman's shoulder. She thought sometimes she had been drawn to rescue work as a way to combat the feeling of helplessness Melissa was experiencing now.

Austen and Ryan emerged from the canyon, where they had been running rope lines, and Sheri rejoined them and the others. "It's a nice, easy slope," Ryan said. "The snow's packed enough you can walk right down."

"Did you hear anything from the van?" Carrie asked.

Ryan grimaced. "I heard kids crying. Don't know if they're hurt or just scared."

"We're going to get some shovels and picks and follow you back down," Austen said.

Hannah and Sheri started down. Ryan was right. They were able to walk down, like walking down a ramp, holding on to the rope for balance. Only the roof of the white van was visible, buried in the snow, the top of the boulder it rested against barely poking above the sea of white. Past the boulder the drop-off was dizzying, hundreds of yards of emptiness to jagged rocks below. Sheri fought a wave of nausea and forced her gaze back to the van. Austen and Ryan followed and began attacking the wall of snow around the vehicle with picks and shovels.

"Hello!" Sheri shouted. "Hang on tight and we're coming to get you!"

A clamor rose from the van, a sound like a beehive suddenly disturbed. The words were mostly unintelligible, though Sheri thought she heard "Help!" and "Thank God!"

The men carved a path to the rear of the van. Faces appeared at the fogged window. "Do you see a red handle?" Hannah called. "Press down on that and see if you can open the window."

Moments later, the window popped open, then fell away, and two girls immediately climbed out into the snow. "Whoa! Whoa!" Sheri moved to block any more exits. "Wait a minute and let's do this safely." She switched on her headlamp, leaned her head and shoulders into the emergency exit and surveyed the scene. Half a dozen pairs of eyes stared back at her, some frightened, a few more curious. "Who are the adults here?" she asked.

"I'm Coach Dellafield." A woman with curly sandy hair and freckles moved down the aisle, holding on to the seat backs to pull herself along the angled floor. "The driver, Mr. Fox, has a bad bump on his head and he's trapped by the seat belt," she said. "One of the girls may have broken her arm. I think everyone else is okay."

Relief surged through Sheri. That was great news.

"Give us a few minutes and we'll have you out of here," she said, and withdrew.

"I heard," Hannah, who had been standing right behind her, said. "Let's get everyone mobile out and I'll go in and see to the driver."

"How stable is this van?" Sheri asked Ryan.

"It's wedged solid against that boulder and the snow is like a mold, holding it in," Ryan said. "For the time being, you're as good as it gets."

She looked past him, to where the two girls who had climbed out stood. They wore light jackets and track pants and hopped up and down in an attempt to keep warm. "We're going to have some people lead you up to the road," she said. "You do exactly what they tell you to do."

"Yes, ma'am," they said, meek now that they were out in the open, perhaps struck by how lucky they had been to avoid a much more serious accident.

Five more girls climbed out of the van and joined the procession to the top, walking up like climbing stairs. Then Hannah and Sheri entered the van and approached Ms. Dellafield, who sat in the aisle near the front of the van with an ashen-faced girl with black braids who cradled her arm. "I need to take a look at that arm," Hannah said gently. "I know it probably hurts to move it, but if I put it in a splint, you'll soon feel much better."

Eyes brimming with tears, the girl allowed Hannah to examine her arm while Sheri moved past them to the driver. Blood stained his Eagle Mountain Eagles sweatshirt and matted his graying hair, but he was conscious. Sheri introduced herself and took his pulse. A little fast, but steady. "What's your name?" she asked.

"Hank Fox."

"What happened, Mr. Fox?"

"We were on our way home from a basketball tournament in Durango. We had just come over the summit and I saw a few chunks of ice hit the road in front of me. I braked—but gently. I know better than to slam on the brakes up here. I mainly tapped the brakes to warn the driver I knew was behind me. The next thing I know we're swamped in this cloud of white. I didn't even have time to steer before we were carried over the edge. The van tilted and I was thrown sideways and bashed my head. I must have blacked out for a few seconds. The next thing I knew, everything went still. I couldn't see anything but white. Someone yelled that we were buried alive and I tell you, that set everyone off. I realized about that time that I had blood all over me and I panicked and started yelling." He made a face. "I'm sure that didn't help calm things down." He tried to look around, but the seat belt held him tight against the seat. "How are the girls?"

"Everyone is fine. One girl with a possible broken arm, but looks like you're the most seriously injured."

"It's just a bump on the head," he said. "I'll be fine."

Hannah moved up to join them. "I put a splint

on Schuyler's arm and Mrs. Delafield and Austen are going to help her walk up to the top," she said. "They're sending down a litter for Mr. Fox."

Sheri moved aside to allow Hannah to examine the van driver, then exited the van altogether when Ted and Eldon arrived with the litter and tools to cut away the safety belt and free Mr. Fox from the vehicle. She returned up top in time to see several of the girls reunited with frantic parents who had learned of the accident from friends or neighbors and driven up to learn the fate of their daughters. This time, the news was all good.

Sheri sat on the back bumper of the Beast and watched as dads and daughters hugged and moms and daughters wept. These parents had feared the very worst—their children being taken from them—and now knew the joy of having their children returned, safe. Even Schuyler, cradling her injured arm, was smiling now, surrounded by family and friends, a momentary celebrity who would emerge from this with a story she would tell for the rest of her life.

Carrie sat on the bumper next to Sheri. "I meant to ask," Sheri said. "Did they figure out why the Beast wasn't running the other night?"

Carrie shook her head. "Just temperamental, I guess. The poor thing only has almost three hundred thousand miles on it. It's long overdue to be replaced, but that will take a major fundraising drive. Probably sooner rather than later, so get ready."

Sheri nodded. Fundraising wasn't her favorite part of search and rescue work, but it was necessary.

Carrie watched as a mom and dad loaded one of the basketball players into their car. "I dread calls like this," she said. "Anything with children ties me in knots. I can't help but think of my own kids." Carrie had a son and daughter, both in elementary school. Sheri had forgotten that. Carrie glanced at her. "They say being a mom makes you tough, but you don't hear very often about how vulnerable it makes you, also."

Sheri nodded. She thought about telling Carrie that she had had a daughter, too. She knew all about that vulnerability. But she didn't say anything. That was a part of herself she didn't talk about.

"Every time we get a call with children involved, I tell myself I'm going to have to give this up," Carrie continued. "I almost quit last spring, after that ATV rollover on Spark Mountain Road."

That accident had involved an ATV with a mom and dad and their two children that had taken a curve too fast and rolled down the mountain. The parents had survived the accident but both children had been killed. Sheri had been in Denver visiting family when it happened and had been relieved not to be involved. "That must have been traumatic for everyone involved," she said.

Carrie nodded. "I saw a counselor for a couple of months afterward. I thought about quitting but the next time a call went out—no kids that time—I had to go, you know? It's like, I'm addicted to rescue work."

Sheri knew. The adrenaline rush, the high when a rescue went well and some innate need to well, *be needed*, all combined to keep a certain kind of person coming back time after time to endure all the hardships and sometimes disappointments of search and rescue work. They had all attended a lecture once by a psychologist who had studied search and rescue volunteers. He told them that success in the field required a positive mental attitude in the face of danger and extreme difficulty. It was the same trait that allowed some people to survive grave injuries or terrible ordeals when all the odds said they wouldn't make it. Sheri would have never said she possessed that kind of attitude, but she supposed when it came down to it, she did.

"Tonight was good," Sheri said. "Everyone is going to be all right." She squeezed Carrie's arm. "Us, too."

Carrie nodded, and stood. "Come on. We'd better load up and get home."

They helped the others gather their equipment and stow it in the Beast. The road crew had freed Melissa Sheffield's vehicle and she had driven away, and the plows cleared the rest of the snow. The road reopened and the law enforcement vehicles left. The SAR crew returned to headquarters, then dispersed to their own homes. Sheri drove to her place, wondering if a glass of wine and a movie would be enough to help her settle down and sleep.

A familiar Jeep was parked in her driveway. As she emerged from her vehicle, the driver's door opened and Erik got out and moved toward her. "I heard about the accident up on the pass," he said. "I heard it was kids." He searched her face, and worry etched the lines around his eyes and mouth deeper.

"It was kids," she said. "But everyone is okay."

"Thank God." He held out his arms and she went to him. She didn't want to want him this way, but she was so glad he was here. She didn't have to tell him what she felt or why. She didn't have to keep quiet about Claire or pretend there wasn't a hole in her heart where her daughter had been. Erik knew her in a way no one else did, and for now that was enough.

SHERI WAS CLEANING her bathroom Saturday morning when the doorbell sounded over Adele blaring from a smart speaker in the adjacent bedroom. It took a few more seconds for the sounds to register and by this time whoever was out there was pounding on the door. She stripped off her rubber gloves, silenced the music and hurried to check the door. She was startled to see Melissa Sheffield looking back at her, the other woman's expression hidden by a pair of oversize sunglasses.

Sheri unlocked and opened the door. "Mrs. Sheffield?"

"May I come in?"

"Of course." Sheri stepped back and Melissa, dressed in high-heeled black boots, a slim black maxi skirt and a long black puffer coat, moved past her into the living room. "Can I get you something?" Sheri asked. "Tea, or I could make coffee."

Melissa took off her gloves, tugging carefully at each finger. When she turned to Sheri, her eyes were bloodshot, devoid of makeup. "I've done something very bad," she said. "I did it for the right reasons, but still." She made a helpless gesture with her hands.

"What do you want me to do?" Sheri asked. "I mean, shouldn't you go to the sheriff's office and tell them? Or, I don't know, a priest or something?"

"I came to you because you seem sympathetic, and because, well, I need rescuing. That's what you do, isn't it? Search and rescue?"

The dazed expression Melissa wore worried Sheri. "Why don't you take off your coat and have a seat," she said.

Melissa hesitated, then moved to the sofa. She sat on the edge of the cushions, knees together, hands folded primly in her lap. Sheri sat beside her, the space of one cushion between them. "My brother needs help," Melissa said. "I've always been the one to help him. That's all I was trying to do this time. I need you to make the law enforcement officers believe that."

"What did you do?" Sheri asked, a knot forming in her stomach.

"Dawn was never in any danger," Mel continued.

"It's been very upsetting for people to ever believe that she was. Carl is not a violent person. He simply isn't. And he loves Dawn. And she's a very…resilient child. She'll take all of this in stride…eventually."

The bad feeling in Sheri's stomach and chest was growing. "What will Dawn understand?" she asked. "What exactly have you done?"

"Carl needed money for his legal expenses," she continued. "Because of these horrible accusations against him, he'd lost his job. He had to be able to defend himself, so he asked Brand and I for the money. It wasn't an unreasonable request. We're his family and families support one another." She pressed her lips together, the lines around her mouth deepening, making her look older and more severe. "Brand refused. I couldn't believe it. It's not as if I'm an extravagant person who goes around wasting his money on silly impulses. I was asking for the money for my brother. For family. But he refused to give Carl one dime."

"What did you do?" Sheri asked again, trying to remain calm. She thought she knew what was coming, but she needed to hear it from Melissa's own lips.

"Brand loves Dawn. I do, too, but sometimes I think she's the only person he truly does love. He's certainly not close to his siblings the way I am to Carl. Carl and I realized that if Dawn was kidnapped, Brand would pay anything to get her back." She glanced at Sheri, clearly annoyed. "No one was supposed to know Carl was the kidnapper, but you ruined that when you spotted him with Dawn at the ice festival. I really think that if it had been anyone but Carl, Brand would have paid the money with no fuss." She sighed. "I don't know why he has to be so difficult. This could have all been over with so much sooner."

Sheri stared at Melissa, questions tumbling over themselves in her head like clothes in a dryer: What kind of mother thought setting her daughter up to be kidnapped—even a pretend kidnapping—was a good idea? Why ask for a million dollars? If Carl was so great, why had he ever agreed to such an outrageous plan? And are you out of your mind?

The question she asked was: "So you weren't worried about your daughter?" Had all that motherly concern and tears been fake?

"Dawn is fine. She's crazy about Carl, and I know he wouldn't let anything happen to her."

Sheri remembered the little girl who had grabbed onto her at the ice festival, and the way she had said, "I want my mom." And the note she had found in the cabin at the closed summer camp. *My uncle is taking me to Mexico and I don't want to go.* "Were you the one who picked up Carl and Dawn when he sent his car into the canyon?" Sheri asked.

"Yes. He wasn't very happy with me that day. Carl really loved that car. But I pointed out with a million dollars, he could buy all the cars he wanted. I had checked out the fishing cabins ahead of time— I knew he and Dawn would be safe there. But he called me that night and told me the woman who ran the place had seen Dawn—which wasn't supposed to happen—and I decided to move them to the summer camp. Not as comfortable, but it would do for a few nights while I worked on Brand."

"Did you puncture Detective Lester's tires?"

Melissa looked her in the eye, completely calm. "I have no idea what you're talking about."

Sheri was sure she was lying, but that didn't really matter, because she believed Melissa was telling the truth about everything else. "Where did you take them after the summer camp?" she asked.

"That's what I need to tell the sheriff," Melissa said. "This has gone on too long. Dawn is very unhappy with me and I need to make it up to her. I'll find a way to make it up to Carl, too. But it's time for this to stop."

Sheri walked to the door and made sure the lock was turned. She didn't want Melissa leaving. She took out her phone. "I'll call Erik," she said.

"I don't want to talk to him," Melissa said. "I want to talk to the sheriff."

"Fine, then I'll call the sheriff." She would text Erik. She wasn't about to leave him out of all of this.

Chapter Twelve

When Sheri told Erik that the person trapped in the second vehicle on Dixon Pass was Melissa Sheffield, he wanted to bring Dawn's mother in for questioning again. But he decided to wait. He would have more leverage to pressure her if he could find someone else connected to Carl who could speak to his intentions. Maybe Carl had mentioned his plan to get money from his brother-in-law to a former coworker or a woman he had dated. And there was the bank account to investigate, too. Erik had put in a request to the FBI for help tracking down the bank associated with the account and needed to follow up on that. Melissa could wait a little while longer.

He devoted himself to contacting Carl Westover's former coworkers, neighbors and known associates and questioning them about a former girlfriend whose name began with *M*, and any trips to Mexico or New Mexico. He asked about foreign bank accounts, and if Carl had ever mentioned wanting to get back at his brother-in-law for refusing to help him.

"Carl was the kind of person who talked big but didn't ever do anything," a former coworker told Erik. "He was mad at his brother-in-law, but the threats, if you could call them that, were more along the lines of 'he'll be sorry he ever treated me this way.'"

"What did he say, exactly?" Erik asked.

"Oh, he said a lot of things, but he was just blowing hot air."

"Can you remember anything specific?"

The man thought for a moment. "Well, okay. One time—last time I saw him, in fact — he said he was going to show Brandon. When Carl ended up more famous and richer than Brandon ever thought about, he'd come crawling to Carl to help him, and Carl would throw him out. See what I mean—a lot of hot air."

"Did he ever talk about his niece, Dawn?" Erik asked.

"Not that I remember. The only family I ever heard him mention was his sister."

"What did he say about her?"

"Oh, just that she had promised to help him fight the charges against him and prove he was innocent. I know they talked a lot on the phone and seemed close."

"Unnaturally close?" Erik asked.

"No. Nothing like that. I think he looked up to her."

Erik thanked the man and hung up the phone. To

some people, *famous* and *notorious* were synonymous. Kidnapping was one way to get your name in the news, but it seemed a stretch to cite Carl's conversation with his old coworker as evidence that he had been planning to abduct his niece for some time.

He checked the clock. It was getting late, and so far he had accomplished nothing today. Time to contact Melissa and find out what she had to say about her activities yesterday. He tried her cell phone number, but got no answer, so he called the phone at their home. Brandon answered.

"I don't know where Melissa is," Brandon said after Erik asked for Melissa. "Her car is gone."

"How long has she been gone?" Erik asked.

"I woke up this morning and she wasn't here. I didn't worry at first. She left a note saying she couldn't sleep and she was going out driving. She does that sometimes. She says it helps her think. But that was hours and hours ago and I haven't heard anything." His voice broke and it was a long moment before he continued. "Do you think Carl took her, too?"

"Has Carl threatened to kidnap your wife, also?" Erik asked.

"No, but what else could have happened to her? She's never stayed away all day like this—not without telling me where she was going ahead of time."

"Have you tried calling her?"

"Several times. All my calls go straight to voice mail."

"Was your wife at home last night?" Erik asked.

"Yes. We went to bed together at eleven."

"Did the two of you argue? Maybe she left this morning because she was angry, and that's why she's not answering your calls."

The man on the other end of the line didn't speak for several seconds. "Mr. Sheffield? Are you still there?"

"I'm here. Melissa and I argue all the time lately. She's angry that I won't hand over money to Carl every time he holds out his hand and she isn't one to hide her feelings. But we didn't talk about that last night. When we said good-night she gave no indication that she was any more upset with me than she has been."

Erik remembered those days—terrible arguments interspersed with attempts to pretend everything was normal. But those efforts always felt perfunctory, even desperate, with no real warmth behind them. He and Sheri hadn't been able to find their way back to the closeness that had once characterized their marriage. "Did Melissa go out yesterday afternoon or evening?" he asked.

Another pause, then, "Yes. She went out for a few hours."

"What time?"

"She left about five o'clock."

"And how long was she gone?"

"Three hours. When she got home she said she

had to wait while the highway crew cleared an avalanche up on Dixon Pass."

"Did she say where she had been, that she was on the other side of Dixon Pass?"

"She said she was trying to find Dawn." His voice broke. "Detective, are we ever going to see our little girl again? I dreamed last night we were attending her funeral. You don't think that was a premonition, do you?"

"I don't believe in premonitions," Erik said. He had lived the hell of attending his child's funeral and no dream could have prepared him for that moment. Neither he nor Sheri had had any warning that Claire would be taken from them. "And we haven't seen anything to indicate that Carl has done anything to harm your daughter," he added.

"You're right. I can't give up hope. Do you want me to come to the station and file some kind of missing persons report on Melissa?"

"I think it's too soon for that. Keep trying her phone, and let us know as soon as she gets home."

"All right."

Erik ended the call and looked up to find the sheriff standing in the doorway. "I heard part of that," Travis said. "And I saw the report about Melissa Sheffield being caught in the avalanche last night. What is she playing at?"

"I don't know," Erik said. "I've been suspicious of Melissa for a while now. I wonder if she's in this with her brother—the two of them teaming up to extort money from her husband. It would explain who has been helping him move around."

"She has alibis for at least some of the times when Carl was being driven from place to place," Travis said.

"You and I both know alibis can be faked." Find the right person to lie for you, or rearrange the facts just slightly to be in your favor. "From my time spent investigating Carl, I know he's a skilled manipulator. I suspect his sister shares his talent."

"It's getting late," Travis said. "Go home and sleep on it. See if any new ideas come to you."

What he wanted was to see Sheri. She was home to him—she always had been. Finding her again had made him realize how true that was. He had believed all the emptiness inside him was because they had lost Claire. He would always mourn his daughter, but the space he had been trying to fill was the one where Sheri belonged. He only hoped he could make her see that, too.

Erik had just pulled into the driveway of his rental when his phone pinged. He smiled when he saw the message was from Sheri, then the smile changed to anger as he read the text: Melissa Sheffield is at my house now. She says she helped her brother and knows where he is now. She wants to talk to the sheriff. I think you should come, too.

His phone rang with a call from the sheriff as Erik was composing his reply. "I just heard from Sheri Stevens," Travis said. "Melissa Sheffield showed up at her house a few minutes ago to confess that she and her brother have been working together."

"Sheri texted me the same." Erik stood. "I want to be there when you question Melissa."

"Meet me there. I'll have a couple of deputies wait outside the house, in case we decide to take her into custody."

Erik backed his Jeep out of the driveway, mind racing. So he had been right to suspect Melissa had helped her brother, but he still couldn't understand why she would do such a thing. Why arrange for your own daughter to be kidnapped. Money? Revenge? He shook his head to clear it. None of that really mattered right now. The question they needed Melissa to answer was where Carl and Dawn were now. They needed to bring the girl home, or to some place she would be safe.

MELISSA REFUSED SHERI'S offers of tea and wine, preferring to pace, still wearing her puffy coat, though the house wasn't cold. She examined the books on Sheri's shelves and the decorative items on her tables with the air of a woman who was shopping at a store she didn't like. Sheri tried asking her more questions—about Carl, about Dawn, about what she thought would happen next, but was greeted with only silence or "I don't want to talk about that."

When lights swept across the front windows as a car pulled into the driveway, relief surged through Sheri and she hurried to look out. Sheriff Travis

Walker moved into the glow from the front porch, bareheaded and wearing a leather jacket with a shearling collar. Behind him was Erik in his black parka.

She unfastened the locks and pulled open the door, wanting to throw her arms around both of them, but settling for "Thank you for coming."

Melissa had finally shed the coat and sat on the edge of the sofa, posed like an elegant statue, knees together, hands folded, head up. She wore a maroon cowl-necked sweater that looked expensive, the deeply rolled collar accentuating the fine bones of her face. She looked beautiful and vulnerable, not the sort of woman who would use her own daughter as a pawn in a sick game to get money for her brother.

Erik and Travis sat on chairs across from her, while Sheri took another chair, out of the circle they made. "I understand you have some things you want to tell us," he said.

"Yes," Melissa answered.

Travis removed a small recorder from his jacket pocket and set it on the table between them. Then he recited the Miranda warning Sheri had heard on countless television episodes and told Melissa he was recording everything. Melissa eyed the recorder like a mouse might view a trap, but indicated she understood her rights. She smoothed her hands, carefully manicured with pearl pink polish, down her thighs and began to talk.

She told them everything she had told Sheri, filling in details as Travis asked for them.

"Why a million dollars?" Travis asked. "When Carl had requested only a hundred thousand before?"

"I know that sounds like an outrageous sum to a lot of people," Melissa said. "But a million dollars hardly makes a dent in Brand's fortune. In addition to the money he's made from his software company, he inherited quite a lot from his grandparents, and will get even more when his parents die. Carl and I come from a much more modest background. In addition to his legal fees, Carl will need money to start over once his name is cleared. He would like to start his own business. Instead of asking Brand for more money then, why not get it all up front? And as I was telling Sheri earlier, this was supposed to be an anonymous crime. Brand wasn't supposed to know who had Dawn. A million sounded like a sum an experienced kidnapper would ask for, don't you think?" She tilted her head to one side, a coquettish gesture that sent a shiver up Sheri's spine.

Erik shifted in his chair, but remained silent, his eyes fixed on Melissa, revealing nothing of his thoughts. Sheri had resented his ability to hide his feelings so well when they were married, but she saw its usefulness now. "Your husband told us your car never left the driveway the day your brother dumped his car," Travis said. "Was he lying?"

"Brand is a terrible liar—he was telling the truth. I told him I was going for a walk, then borrowed a neighbor's car. I told her the battery in mine had died and we were waiting for the road service to deliver a new one, but that in the meantime I needed to get something from the store. She didn't question me, just handed over the keys. People here are very trusting and helpful."

She managed to make something good sound like a fault. "How did your daughter react when she saw you?" Erik spoke for the first time, asking a question Sheri had wondered about also.

"Dawn was happy to see me. I told her she was going to stay with Uncle Carl a little while longer but they would have a good time together and we would be back together soon."

"And she accepted that?" Erik asked.

"She whined that she wasn't having a good time, but children are like that. Easily bored. I reassured her. After all, I'm her mother."

You don't deserve her, Sheri thought, but said nothing.

"Where did you take your brother and your daughter after they left the summer camp?" Travis asked.

"There's a group of summer cabins in the national forest up there somewhere," Melissa said. "I found it when I was driving around. I told Carl he would be safe in that spot and that I would bring him some more food and supplies today, but when I went up there this afternoon, he was gone. That's when I decided I had to come clean. If he's not going to cooperate with me, I wasn't going to help him anymore."

"So you didn't pick up Carl and Dawn and take them to another location?" Travis asked.

"No. When I got to the cabin, they were gone. I can show you where it is if you like." She leaned forward. "I'm really worried about them. Carl is a very capable man, very smart, but he's not an outdoorsman. He's the type who'll get lost in the woods. He doesn't like hiking, or being cold, or doing any of the things he must have had to do after he left that hiding place."

"Do you have any idea where he might have gone?" Travis asked.

"None. I'm completely in the dark."

Travis stood. "We need you to come to the station now."

Melissa stared up at them, wide-eyed, somehow looking younger than her years. "Am I under arrest?"

"Not at this time, but we want to talk to you more about your brother's motive and possible next move."

"I'm always happy to help the police," she said. "Though I'll want to contact my lawyer."

"You can call your attorney from the sheriff's department."

"You can contact your husband, too," Erik said. "He's been very worried about you."

"I don't want to talk to Brand right now," Melissa said. "He's already so upset about Dawn. He wouldn't understand that what happened was just a…a prank that got out of hand."

Sheri had trouble not gaping at the woman. Kidnapping a child and trying to extort a million dollars was not a "prank."

"When we do find Carl, we may need you to persuade him to give himself up and release your daughter unharmed," Travis said. "We hope you can help us with that. Will you talk to him?"

"Of course." She stood, her smile still in place, though Sheri thought it looked a little harder. "Carl will listen to me. He always has."

MELISSA BALKED AT riding with Travis in his SUV, but he ignored her protests. "I'll have a deputy pick up your car later," he said.

"Will he be coming along, too?" Melissa asked, indicating Erik.

"Detective Lester will follow in his own vehicle."

Melissa folded her arms over her chest. "I'm not going to get into any car with a man who is a stranger to me," she said. "I've heard too many stories about what can happen to a woman who does something like that."

Travis's jaw tightened. Erik half expected him to tell Melissa that in that case, she was under arrest, but Sheri spoke up. "I'll come with you," she said. She moved closer to Melissa. "I'm sure Mrs. Sheffield would feel more comfortable with another woman along. Someone who understands what she's going through."

"Yes." Melissa looked grateful and took Sheri's hand. "That would make me feel better."

Erik caught Sheri's eye and read the revulsion behind her feigned sympathy. Like him, Melissa Sheffield's actions disgusted her. But also like him, Sheri would do anything to help Melissa's daughter.

"I need to search you and make sure you aren't carrying a weapon," Travis said.

"That's outrageous," she protested.

"Standard procedure," Travis said.

"I'll do it," Erik said. She already loathed him, and he didn't care what she thought. Melissa could play the distraught mother card all she wanted, but considering the crimes she had already confessed to, he wouldn't put it past her to be armed. "Arms up, legs apart," he ordered. "This will only take a moment."

She was ready to make a fuss, but Sheri put a hand on her arm. "Remember, this is for Dawn," she said.

Melissa clenched her jaw, but nodded, and allowed him to pat her down. "No weapon," he said when he was done.

She glared at him as Sheri walked with her to Travis's SUV. The two women climbed in the back seat and when he was sure they were settled, Erik headed for his Jeep. He would have preferred to have Sheri ride with him, but he appreciated how she was helping them manage Melissa. He and Travis were on the same page when it came to treating Dawn's mother with kid gloves, for the time being. If they could keep her in a cooperative mood, they had a better chance of learning everything she knew about

Carl's whereabouts and plans. Justice would come for her soon enough, but right now saving a child took priority.

NO ONE SPOKE on the short ride to the sheriff's department. Sheri watched Melissa out of the corner of her eye, trying to read her mood, and failing. Before tonight, she had projected her own feelings onto the other woman. She had believed that Melissa must be as distressed over her daughter's abduction as Sheri would have been. Part of her shock now came from realizing she had been so wrong.

At the sheriff's department, Travis and a deputy escorted Melissa to a small gray room furnished only with a table and two chairs. Melissa glanced around the space, lip curled as if she had tasted sour milk. "I'd prefer to wait in the lobby," she said.

"Here will be fine," Travis said. "I'll have someone bring you a phone. Ms. Stevens, come with me."

They left Melissa with the deputy. Erik met them in the hall. "While Mrs. Sheffield talks to her lawyer, you and I can interview Ms. Stevens," Travis said. "Take her into Interview B and I'll meet you in five."

Erik led the way to a room identical to the one in which they had left Melissa. Sheri told herself she had nothing to be nervous about, but the stark room and Travis's characterization of this as a formal interview had her on edge. Erik said nothing until the door closed behind them, then he turned to her. "Are you okay?"

"Yes." She hugged her arms to her chest. "I'm having a hard time wrapping my head around a mother doing that to her child."

He slipped his arm around her and pulled her close. "You've been a big help with her so far."

The door opened and Erik moved away again as Travis entered the room. "I have two deputies with Mrs. Sheffield," he said. "I'm sure she's already telling her attorney how poorly she's being treated." He gestured to the table. "Let's sit and you can tell us what she told you."

Erik sat next to Sheri, facing Travis across the table. His presence steadied her as she related everything Melissa had told her. "So her story is that she drove to the summer cabins where Carl and Dawn were supposedly staying, and they weren't there?" Travis asked. "He had just walked away?"

"That's what she said." Sheri twisted her hands together. "She said he wasn't an outdoorsman. She was afraid he would get lost and that's what prompted her to confess to me."

"Why you?" Travis asked.

"I don't know, really. I suppose it's because I'm another woman and until now, I've been sympathetic to her?"

"Or because she thought she could manipulate you into sympathizing with her actions," Erik said.

"Where are these summer cabins?" Travis asked.

"She didn't say."

"There are several groups of cabins like that in

the county," Travis said. "We'll have to look at a map and pinpoint those closest to the camp where they last stayed, then send deputies to check for any signs Carl and Dawn were there."

"They may have been there, but if they left, I doubt it was because Carl decided to strike out on his own," Erik said. "He's had big sister chauffeuring him all over the county for the last few days. Why set out on foot now, especially since she indicated he was expecting her to pick him up?"

"Maybe something spooked him," Travis said.

"Or Melissa is lying." Erik angled toward Sheri. "Did she say anything to indicate she knows where Carl is now?"

"No. She says she doesn't know."

"What's her motive for lying?" Travis asked.

"She realizes we're closing in and wants to distance herself from her brother," Erik said.

"So she's helped him all this time and now she's cutting him loose?" Travis asked. "And then she readily admits her part in the crime. It feels like something is missing from this story."

"I think Melissa knows where Carl is, but she thinks if she keeps stonewalling we'll find him on our own," Erik said. "Then she can plead that he manipulated her into helping him and that, ultimately, he's mostly responsible for everything that happened."

"Huh." Travis turned his attention to Sheri. "Did Melissa say anything else you haven't told us yet?"

"No. Except…" She bit her lower lip, hesitating.

"What is it?" Erik asked.

"It wasn't anything she said, it's just… If I thought I knew where my daughter was and suddenly I didn't—if it was possible she was lost in the woods—I'd be frantic. Melissa is a little nervous. She's impatient and irritated. But she isn't scared. And she's scarcely mentioned Dawn. That feels off to me."

"Some people are more reserved than others," Travis said. "But I see your point." He stood. "I'm going to have Gage search for cabins where Carl and Dawn might have been, then I'll meet you in Interview B. Let's see if Melissa has anything more to say. Ms. Stevens, I can have someone take you home."

"Would it be all right if I stayed here for a while?" Sheri asked. "Maybe I could be useful, since Melissa seems comfortable with me."

Travis nodded. "Suit yourself. But you could be here a while."

He left the room and Sheri turned to Erik. "It's not as if I would get any sleep at home," she said. "What is going to happen to Melissa?"

"She'll be charged, eventually," Erik said. "Right now we want her to tell us as much as she can, and help us find Dawn. If she believes we're sympathetic, and willing to go easy on her, the chances are greater that she'll cooperate."

"Do you think this is all a game to her?" Sheri asked. "When she was telling me everything that had happened, before you and Travis arrived, I got the sense that she was almost proud that she had orchestrated everything so well. She didn't have any qualms about trying to trick her husband into handing over a million dollars to her brother. What kind of marriage is that?"

"Not the kind I want." His eyes met hers. She saw his fatigue there, and sadness. "Not the kind we ever had, even at our worst." He stood. "Come on. You can wait in the space I'm using as an office. I'll get you some coffee and you can make yourself at home. I think the sheriff was right—it's going to be a long night."

Chapter Thirteen

Melissa sat at the conference room table, legs and arms crossed, one foot moving in time to some rhythm only she could hear. When Travis and Erik entered, she jumped up. "My attorney has advised me not to talk to you until he arrives," she said.

"When will that be?" Travis asked.

"Not before tomorrow, I imagine. He has to drive over from Denver." She smiled. "Why don't we all go home and we can meet to discuss this tomorrow."

"What about Dawn?" Erik asked.

The smile vanished. "What about her?"

"Aren't you concerned about where she might be?" Erik moved to stand in front of her. "You said you thought Carl had left the cabin with her and could be lost."

"I'm assuming you're going to be looking for them," she said.

"Where is this cabin where you say you left them last?" Travis asked.

"I don't think it has an address," she said. "But

I'm sure you'll be able to find it. It's not far from the King's Kids camp—in that same general area, off one of those forest service side roads."

"Could you take us there?" he asked.

"I'm sure I could, though I can't promise I could find it in the dark."

"Is there really a cabin?" Erik asked. "Or did you make up that story so we would intensify our search for your brother in that area?"

"You keep reassuring me you're doing everything you can to find my little girl. Are you saying that's not the case? Why should I resort to made-up stories to get you to do your job?" She turned to the sheriff. "Do you have people looking for Carl and Dawn, or not?"

"I have people looking for them." He pulled out one of the chairs. "Have a seat."

"No. I want to go home."

"You need to wait here for a bit," he said.

"Wait for what? I've had enough of this. I want to go home." She started for the door. Erik knew there were two deputies stationed outside who would stop her if she tried to leave, but before she could try that, the door opened and Brandon Sheffield burst in. "Mel, are you all right?" He gripped her shoulders. "I came as soon as the sheriff called to tell me you were being questioned."

"I'm fine." Melissa shrugged out of his grasp. "You're just in time to take me home. I'm exhausted."

"Your wife has admitted to helping her brother to

abduct your daughter in order to extort money from you," Travis said.

Brandon gaped at him.

"*Abduct* is a very inflammatory word," Melissa said. "As is *extort*."

Brandon stared at her. "What is he talking about?" he asked.

"Carl needed that money and you were wrong to refuse to help him," she said. "He came up with a very simple plan to get the money and I agreed to help. If you had paid up, Dawn wouldn't have been away for more than one night at most, and you know how much she enjoys spending time with Carl, so you see how that really isn't an abduction, don't you?" She turned to Travis. "And the whole thing was really Carl's idea. I only agreed to go along to protect Dawn."

"You have a funny way of protecting your daughter," Erik said. So much for keeping her cooperative. He'd had more than enough of her pretending she was innocent.

"You *helped* Carl?" Brandon asked. "To kidnap our daughter and hold her for ransom?"

"I'm not going to say another word until my lawyer gets here," she said. "Except that you can't believe everything they tell you." She nodded to the sheriff. "He's trying to paint me as some monster and I'm not. And Dawn is fine and has been this whole time."

Brandon took a step toward her. "You took our

daughter away from her home and kept her away in order to what—teach me a lesson? Extract revenge? You thought your brother's greed was more important than our child's well-being?"

She backed away. "I told you not to listen to them," she said. "And if you had given Carl the money he asked for to begin with, this never would have happened, so you're every bit as much to blame as I am."

Brandon lunged toward her. Travis and a deputy pulled him off. "I'm sorry," he said. "I'll control myself." He sent his wife a look of loathing. "Where is Dawn now?" he asked. "Do you know?"

She said nothing, merely shook her head. Brandon turned to Travis. "We're searching for your daughter now," the sheriff said. "We're hoping Mrs. Sheffield will tell us if she knows where they are. She's indicated she believes your daughter and her brother may be lost in the woods somewhere."

"It's twenty degrees out there!" he said, his voice rising. "There's two feet of snow on the ground. Melissa! If you know where they are, tell us!"

A knock on the door interrupted. The deputy opened the door and Gage leaned in. "There's been a development." He glanced toward Melissa and Brandon.

Travis left the room, Erik behind him. "We got a call about some vandalism up on Marietta Peak," Gage said. "There's a satellite tower up there and the provider has had problems with people stealing the solar batteries that run the transmission equipment.

So they installed an alarm and cameras. The alarm went off about ninety minutes ago. They downloaded footage from the camera and sent it right over to us. I think you ought to see it."

"Why? What's on it?" Travis asked.

"I want you to take a look and draw your own conclusions," Gage said.

They followed Gage to his desk, and leaned over to watch the grainy black-and-white video that played on Gage's laptop screen. "This was taken at night, so the resolution is lousy," Gage said.

Two figures emerged from the shadows and approached the door of a small building—one figure tall and bulky, one very short. The larger figure fumbled at the door, then stepped back and pulled something from his pocket. There was no sound, but Erik recognized the bright flash of gunfire. The second figure, behind the first, raised its hands, as if to cover its ears. Then the first figure shoved against the door. It opened, and the two figures went inside. The clip ended.

Gage straightened. "What do you think?"

"Where is this, exactly?" Erik asked.

"About six miles from the summer camp," Gage said. "There's a good dirt road up there."

"You think it's Carl and Dawn," Erik said.

"Don't you? The sizes are right. Who else is going to be up there with a kid? And stay there? The satellite company is monitoring the camera feed and they say the two of them haven't left."

"Why did they wait ninety minutes to notify us?" Travis asked.

"They had to get a supervisor to look at the footage or something," Gage said. "Then they probably had a meeting to decide whether to handle it themselves or call us in."

Travis shook his head. "What's the building they broke into?" he asked.

"It houses the transmitter, maybe some other things. It's heated and air-conditioned so the equipment doesn't malfunction. There's probably enough room in there to camp out for a night or two. Out of the weather."

"And it's not an obvious hideout," Travis said. He stepped back from the computer. "We need to get up there with a team. A hostage negotiator, for sure."

Gage frowned. "Carl is armed. We don't want to go in with the cavalry and spook him into hurting the kid."

"What are the chances of getting to the tower without him noticing?"

"Close to zero. Nothing is up there but the satellite tower and that building. There's no other reason for anyone to come to that spot and he would hear any vehicle long before it got there. The company that owns the equipment wanted to send some workers to it and I had to impress upon them the stupidity of going anywhere near an armed man who might possibly be holding a hostage."

"We could hike up," Erik said.

"We could." Gage paused. "We've already sent a couple of deputies on foot to watch the place. They're instructed not to confront Carl, but to keep track of him if he and the girl leave."

"What if we get Melissa to talk to Carl?" Travis said. "He and his sister are close. Maybe she can persuade him to give himself up, or at least send the girl out."

"I don't trust Melissa to stick to any script we give her," Erik said. "And Carl may not feel so charitable toward her if he thinks she's betrayed him to us."

"We'll get a professional negotiator up there, too," Travis said. "But I think Melissa has the best chance of getting through to him."

Erik didn't like it, but he also didn't see an alternative. "All right," he said. "I'll do whatever I can to help."

"Contact CBI about a hostage negotiator," Travis said. "Gage, get two more deputies up there to keep eyes on that building, but tell them not to let Carl see them. I'll talk to SWAT." He checked his watch. "Be ready to go in thirty minutes."

SHERI WAS CONTEMPLATING stretching out on the floor or Erik's office space and trying to take a nap when he stuck his head in the door. "Come with me a minute," he said.

"Where are we going?" she asked as she followed him down the hallway.

"We think we've found Carl and Dawn. We're

going to talk to Melissa and I think it would be a good idea if you were there." He glanced at her. "You're the sympathetic ear that will pressure her to do the right thing."

"And what is the right thing?"

"Help us by talking to her brother." He pushed open the door to the room where Melissa waited. Brandon stood against the wall on the opposite side of the room, arms crossed, frowning at his wife, who managed to look serene in spite of the tension that filled the air like fog. The sheriff loomed over her, while a pair of deputies waited on either side of the door.

"Are you familiar with Marietta Peak?" Travis asked Melissa.

She looked up at him. "No. Where is that?"

"Not far from the summer camp where we know Carl and Dawn last stayed," Travis said. "There's some satellite equipment up there, and a building housing equipment. A little less than two hours ago, two people broke into the building. We have the surveillance tapes and we believe the intruders were Carl and Dawn."

"Well, thank God you've found them," Melissa said.

Brandon straightened. "Is it really them? Is Dawn all right?"

"The video is poor quality, but we believe it could be them," Travis said. "Dawn appears to be okay, but again, the quality of the images is poor and we only glimpsed her. We got a better look at the man."

He turned back to Melissa. "Did you know Carl and Dawn were there?"

"Of course not," she said. "I already told you, the last time I saw them was when I dropped them off at that group of summer cabins. Why don't you people believe me?"

Because you've proven you can lie so well, Erik thought.

"What are you going to do?" Brandon asked. "How are you going to rescue my little girl?"

"We want you to come with us to Marietta Peak," Travis said to Melissa. "Tell your brother all of this is over. He needs to release Dawn and turn himself in."

She stood. "Of course. That's what I've wanted ever since I went to Sheri's house. I just want this to be over."

"I'm coming, too," Brandon said.

Travis studied him. "You have to stay back a safe distance and not interfere."

Brandon nodded. "All I want is to take Dawn home once she's safe."

"I want to come, too." Sheri's face heated as everyone turned to look at her, but she forged on. "I'm not a paramedic, but I do have first aid training. I can check Dawn and make sure she's really okay."

"Of course she's okay," Melissa said. "Carl would never hurt her."

"Of course not," Sheri agreed. "But you know how children are—they're always coming down with sore throats or colds. If something like that has happened, I know you'd want Dawn treated right away."

Melissa seemed to consider this, then nodded. "She's right. I want Sheri to come. In the car with me." She gave the sheriff a long look that clearly said she didn't trust him.

"Same instructions for you," Travis told Sheri. "Stay back and don't interfere."

She nodded. "Yes, sir."

A caravan of vehicles left the sheriff's department, the sheriff in the lead with Erik, Melissa and Sheri with him. Two patrol cars with deputies followed, with Brandon Sheffield's SUV behind. As Travis fastened his seat belt, Erik got a call that a hostage negotiator was on the way from Junction.

"Let's let Melissa talk to her brother first," Travis said. "We may not need the negotiator, but keep her on standby."

They drove in silence into the mountains outside town. Whenever Sheri glanced over at Melissa, the other woman was staring out the window at the darkness, her expression unreadable.

Halfway up Marietta Peak, they gathered at a staging area. Half a dozen law enforcement vehicles were parked in the trees, their open doors casting yellow light onto the snow. Men and women in uniform or black SWAT gear milled about in the cold, their breath forming clouds, like speech bubbles with no words. "Are you sure this is out of sight of the building up there?" Erik asked as Travis shut off the engine.

"The tower is on the other side of the peak," Travis said. "And the trees provide cover." He and Erik both got out of the car.

"What about us?" Melissa asked.

"You can wait here," Travis said.

She opened her mouth to argue, but Sheri said, "We can use the time to run through what you're going to say to your brother."

Melissa glared at her. "I don't need to *rehearse*. I'm just going to tell him to give up this silly game. It's time for Dawn to come home."

"You obviously know your brother better than anyone," Sheri said. "How do you think he's going to respond?"

"He'll whine. He'll talk about how none of this is his fault. But he'll know I'm right and in the end he'll do what I tell him. He doesn't like getting on my bad side."

So much for Melissa's contention that Carl had come up with this plan and she had just gone along to protect her daughter. Clearly Melissa was the dominant personality in this relationship. "Does he respond to flattery?" Sheri asked. "Maybe you should start with that—talk about how much he loves Dawn and how you know he only wants what's best for her."

"I think I know how to talk to my own brother. I

don't need your help." She looked around. "Where did the sheriff go?"

"I think he's over there with those other officers." Sheri indicated the group of uniformed men and women at the edge of the spotlight.

"I want to hear what they're talking about." Melissa groped at the door. "How do we get out of here?"

"I don't think we do," Sheri said. "That's the thing about cop cars—you don't get out of the back seat until they let you." She didn't like the idea of being stuck in this vehicle with a woman she was beginning to believe was unbalanced. But she was in this too deep to back out now. This was a second chance for her to save a little girl in danger. Maybe doing so would help assuage some of the guilt she still suffered over Claire's accident.

Whatever happened, none of them were going to come out of this predicament untouched. She only hoped a little girl didn't suffer because of the folly of the adults involved.

ERIK AND TRAVIS met Gage on the edge of the crowd. "Dwight and Shane report no sign of Carl or Dawn," Gage said. "I think they're tucked in for the night. There are no windows in that building. We could probably surround the place without him knowing about it, especially with the darkness for cover."

"Do it," Travis said. "But stay as far back as you can and still have the building well in sight. I'm going to take Melissa closer and get her to talk to Carl."

Erik and Travis returned to the car. Erik opened the back passenger door and Melissa hurried out, pulling her coat tightly around her. "What do you mean, walking off and leaving us trapped back there?" she demanded.

Sheri and Travis came around the car and joined them. "What's going on?" Melissa demanded. "What are we waiting for?"

"Carl and Dawn are in a small building at the top of the peak," Travis said. "We know Carl has a pistol. He used it to shoot the lock off the building. What kind of gun is it?"

Erik expected her to say she didn't know, but Melissa surprised him. "It's a Taurus 9mm," she said. "I didn't like the idea of him having it, but he insisted I buy it for him. But don't worry—he won't use it on you. He's not that kind of man at all."

"We need to get going," Travis said. "It's another mile up to the tower." He glanced at Melissa's high-heeled boots. "Can you make the hike?"

"That won't be necessary." She took out a cell phone. "I can call Carl."

Chapter Fourteen

Erik stared at the phone in Melissa's hand. "That's not the cell phone you were using the other day," he said.

"I bought this so that Carl and I could communicate without anyone knowing," she said. "It should come in handy now."

As soon as she had made her call, Erik planned to seize that phone. No telling what kind of incriminating evidence her phone records would provide.

She punched in a number and waited. When he answered, Carl's agitation was evident, his voice clear despite Melissa's effort to press the phone more tightly to her cheek. "Mel? Mel, where are you? You were supposed to be here hours ago."

So much for her story about having arranged to meet Carl at a summer cabin and his leaving on his own, and her claim that she hadn't known where he was. Carl had clearly expected to rendezvous with her here. "Carl, I'm here on Marietta Peak," she said. "With a lot of sheriff's deputies. You need to give yourself up."

"What are you talking about?" He sounded frantic. "You want me to just turn myself in? What are you doing to me?"

"It's for the best," she said. "How is Dawn?"

"Dawn isn't good. She's sick. I think she's running a fever. All this running around in the cold isn't good for her. I told you—"

"Don't lie, Carl," she chided. "You're terrible at it. I'm sure Dawn will be fine. Send her out of the building and tell her to walk down the road toward the lights."

"I'm not going to send a sick child out into the dark and cold on top of a mountain." Erik was relieved to hear that at least one of this pair had a little sense where the child was concerned.

Melissa sighed. "Fine. Then I'll come and get her." She ended the call. "I guess we're going to have to walk up there after all."

She and Travis started toward the road leading up to the summit. Sheri took a few steps after them, but Erik grabbed her arm to stop her. "You can't go up there," he said.

She pulled her arm away. "You heard him. That little girl is sick. I'm not a paramedic, but I do have basic first aid training. The least I can do is assess her."

He was prepared to tell her all the reasons she had no business getting anywhere near an armed kidnapper when Melissa called back to them. "I want Sheri to

come with us," she said. "At least then I'll have someone up there who is on my side."

Sheri's expression softened. "Don't worry," she
said softly, close enough that maybe Erik was the
only one who heard. Then she strode past him to
join the sheriff and Melissa. He fell into step behind them, prepared to do whatever it took to protect Sheri. She might be used to risking her safety
for others, but he didn't know if he could ever grow
accustomed to standing by and watching while she
put her life on the line.

SHERI FELT ERIK'S gaze burning into her as she hiked
up the mountain just behind the sheriff and Melissa.
The road was snow-packed and rutted, and the sheriff had warned they would be making the climb in
the dark. "We don't want to be a target," he had said.
Melissa had looked alarmed, but Sheri had merely
nodded.

She had made this kind of climb before, up
rougher trails, in worse weather. Lives had been on
the line in those situations, too, but this time everything felt more urgent. If any of them said or did the
wrong thing, Carl might snap and Dawn could be
hurt. Sheri wanted Dawn safe, but how safe would
she be with a mother like Melissa?

Sheri saw the faint outline of the tower against the
moonlit sky first, then the red light blinking steadily
on the top. A concrete cube of a building squatted
at the base of the tower, sides glowing the color of

butter in the moonlight. The sheriff halted them two hundred feet from the tower. Sheri hoped this was out of the range of a pistol shot.

"What should I do now?" Melissa asked.

"Call Carl again," Travis said.

Melissa slipped the phone from her pocket and hit a button. Carl's voice broke the silence. "What is going on out there, Mel? What are you doing?"

"I'm here with the sheriff," Melissa said. "Right outside that little building you're in. Send Dawn out to me."

"And then what?" he asked. "The cops come in and shoot me?"

"They're not going to shoot you," she said. "Once Dawn is safe with me, you'll surrender and we'll get this all sorted out down at the sheriff's department."

"The cops hate me," he said. "They think I'm someone who would harm a child. Why did I let you talk me into this?"

"Don't be ridiculous. This was your idea originally. I just agreed to help."

"That's what you told them, isn't it? Well, you can forget about me sending Dawn back out to you!"

Afraid he was going to hang up, Sheri grabbed the phone from Melissa. "Mr. Westover!" she said. "Please don't hang up. My name is Sheri Stevens. I'm with Eagle Mountain Search and Rescue. I'm not a law enforcement officer. I'm not armed. I don't mean you any harm. But I'm trained to give medical care in the field. Can I come in and check on Dawn, just to reassure you that she's all right? I can tell you're very concerned about her. It's obvious you care about her."

"Is this some kind of trick?" he asked.

"No. I promise it isn't. I'll come by myself. Just me and my medical kit, to take care of Dawn."

He hesitated and she bit her lip, praying he would let her in. She stared at the little building, wishing she could see what was going on in there.

"All right," he said. "But just you. No one else. I have a gun. I don't want to use it, but I will if I have to, to protect myself."

"Understood."

He ended the call. Sheri returned the phone to Melissa. "That's a wonderful idea," Melissa said.

"It's a terrible idea." Erik pulled her around to face him. "You can't do this," he said.

"I have to," she said.

"No you don't. I've been in enough situations like this to know what will happen. I'm beginning to believe that Carl doesn't want to hurt his niece, but you're a stranger to him. You'll make the perfect hostage. He'll try to use you to get what he wants."

"I know." That knowledge ought to frighten her, but it didn't. All she could think of was Dawn. "I have to help that little girl," she said.

"We're all here to help her," Erik said.

"But right now, I'm the only one who can do anything," she said. She leaned closer to him, her voice low, the words urgent. "Please. I couldn't save Claire, but now I have a chance to save Dawn. It's a chance I have to take."

"I agree with Erik," the sheriff said. "Getting involved in this is a bad idea."

"No, this is our best chance," Sheri said. She didn't wait for him to say more, but turned and ran toward the building. By the time the others recovered from their shock and sprinted after her, she was already pounding on the door. "Mr. Westover! Carl! It's Sheri Stevens. Please let me in."

"No!" ERIK SHOUTED AS the door to the building opened and Sheri was pulled inside. The door slammed and he stared at it, anger and terror warring in his chest.

"All we can do now is wait," Travis said. "I'm going to talk to the SWAT commander about strategy." He pulled out his radio and turned away, but before he could make a connection, Brandon Sheffield and two deputies arrived. Brandon ignored the rest of them and headed for his wife. "Melissa, what is going on?" he asked.

"Now is not the time to discuss this," she said. She tried to turn away, but he grabbed her arm and pulled her back.

One of the deputies started to step in, but Travis motioned him back. "Let's see what they have to say."

Erik understood. In the heat of the moment, one or both of them might say something revealing. Something incriminating.

"You could have prevented all of this, if you hadn't been so miserly," Melissa said.

"All of what?" Brandon asked. "Are you trying to justify what Carl did by shifting blame? Because that is going too far."

"You're the one who's gone too far!" she retorted. "Turning down a perfectly reasonable request—"

Travis's phone rang and he answered, then caught Erik's eye. *It's Carl*, he mouthed.

Erik moved closer to listen in. "I'm sending Dawn out," Carl said. "I wanted you to know so you don't do anything stupid like shoot her, thinking it's me."

"No one is shooting anyone," Travis said. "What about Ms. Stevens?"

"She's staying with me. She's my ticket out of here."

"IF YOU WANT DAWN, you're going to have to do things my way." Carl clutched the phone with white-knuckled fingers, and paced back and forth in the small shed. The square building had unfinished sheetrock walls and concrete floors that were crowded with an array of gray metal boxes that hummed and clicked in harmony with the heating unit mounted high on one wall. The constant drone was giving Sheri a headache.

"What's going on?" Beside her, Dawn wiggled closer and whispered in Sheri's ear. Her skin was hot to the touch and her eyes were bright with fever. The thermometer Sheri had pulled from her backpack registered a temperature of 102 degrees. The number had alarmed Carl enough that he had pulled out his phone and called the sheriff and made his offer to release the child, in exchange for Sheri. "Am I going to get to go home?" Dawn asked.

"I hope so." Sheri smoothed the girl's hair, soft as only a child's hair can be. The idea of being stuck in this small space with Carl didn't appeal to her, but she told herself it would be worth it to save this little girl. Carl was still talking to the sheriff, though he had moved farther away from them and another machine had kicked on, its louder whine drowning out his words.

Carl pocketed the phone and came to stand in front of them. "How are you doing, kiddo?" he asked Dawn.

"I don't feel good." She buried her head against Sheri's shoulder. "I want to go home."

"Then that's just where you're going." Carl knelt in front of them. Traces of the confident man Sheri had encountered at the ice festival remained, but the past few days as a fugitive had taken their toll. His eyes were red-rimmed, and a shadow of beard darkened his jaw. He smelled of stale sweat and his skin was pasty. "Give me a hug and then we'll go over to the door. I'll open it and you walk out to the people waiting out there." He touched her shoulder. "I'm sorry you're not feeling well. I was hoping we'd have a better time than this. You know I love you, don't you?"

Dawn nodded, her head rubbing against Sheri's jacket. "I love you, too, but I want my mom."

"Your mom is right outside," Carl said. "So are a lot of other people, but don't let them scare you. Now give me a hug."

She moved away from Sheri and wrapped her uncle in a hug. Carl lingered a moment, his arms around her, then released her and stood, and offered his hand. She took it and he led her to the door. He waited a moment, then slowly pulled it open, staying out of sight behind the door. "Go on, honey," he said to Dawn.

The little girl didn't look back, but took a few steps into the darkness, then began to run.

Carl closed the door and sagged against it, eyes closed. Sheri watched him, wondering what was going through his head right now. People who knew him kept saying he wasn't the violent type, but she could clearly see the bulge of the pistol in a holster at his hip. Was he desperate enough to use it?

He opened his eyes and met her gaze. "You're the woman I met at the ice festival, aren't you?" he asked. "The one who identified me to the cops."

She shifted, uncomfortable sitting on the hard floor, but also uneasy about what those words implied. Was he angry with her for spoiling his plan to remain anonymous? "What happens now?" she asked.

"The sheriff said they're bringing in a negotiator for me to talk to." He slid down the door until he was sitting on the floor with his back to it, knees up.

"I'm sure he or she will try to talk me into turning myself in, but it's too late for that."

"Why do you say that?" Sheri folded her legs under her, trying to get more comfortable. Though the air in the room was warm, cold seeped up through the concrete floor.

"When I was just facing embezzlement charges, it wasn't so bad," he said. "I could have beat those, or made some kind of plea. But kidnapping a kid?" He shook his head. "They'll send me to prison for the rest of my life for that."

"Why did you do it?" she asked.

He blew out a breath. "First of all, I didn't kidnap my niece. Not really. I mean, it's not kidnapping if the parents—well, at least her mom—knew where she was the whole time. That's what Mel told me, anyway. This was all her idea. The plan was that I'd take Dawn with me for a few hours, maybe over-night, and pretend to be a kidnapper. I'd send a text demanding money. Mel would freak out and plead with Brandon to pay the money. He might balk at first, but he would eventually cave. Mel was sure of that. Once the money was safely socked away in the account Mel helped me set up, I'd show up with Dawn and say I found her and everybody would be happy."

"Weren't you worried Dawn would tell police what really happened?"

"Mel promised that wouldn't happen. She said she would explain to Dawn that this was a big secret. She said if Dawn did say anything, Mel would tell them she was just confused. No one would believe a little kid over the word of her own mother."

Sheri wasn't so sure of that, but didn't see the point of mentioning it. "What about the gun?" she asked. "If this was so innocent, why do you have that?"

The lines on either side of his mouth deepened. "Mel bought that gun and insisted I take it. I didn't want to, but she said I might need it to protect myself while Dawn and I were waiting for Brandon to transfer the money. She insisted on it."

Sheri wondered if Mel had done this to make her brother look guiltier. "Melissa told the sheriff everything was your idea," she said. "She insisted you persuaded her to go along."

He slumped farther, wrists resting loosely on his knees. "I guess I ought to be surprised by that, but I'm not. Melissa has always been very good at looking out for number one, for all she's been a big help to me over the years."

"Do you really think the cops will let you walk out of here?" she asked.

"They'll have to. They won't want to risk you getting hurt. I really don't want to hurt you, but as long as I can make them believe I will, I have the upper hand. At least now I know Dawn is safe. I never would have harmed her."

"You should give yourself up," she said. "Tell the

police what you told me. Don't let your sister let you take all the blame."

"Yeah, I tried surrendering once before and that didn't work out so well for me."

"When did you try to surrender?" she asked, confused.

"When they charged me with stealing that money from Western Casing."

"You didn't steal it?"

He grimaced. "I borrowed it. I was going to pay it back."

"How?"

"I'd have found a way. There was no reason to treat me like a criminal. That Detective Lester wouldn't leave me alone. He was constantly questioning me, talking to my neighbors and friends, women I used to date. I thought that kind of harassment was illegal. He just wouldn't let it go."

Erik had always been dogged in his pursuit of justice. It had made him great at his job, though more than once his devotion to his work had made Sheri feel left out. After Claire had died, he had worked endless hours of overtime. She had convinced herself it was because he didn't want to be with her. With time, she had come to see it was his way of trying to outrun grief.

"He's not going to quit pursuing you if you manage to get away," she said.

"He won't know where to find me," Carl said.

"If you leave the country, you'll be an international

fugitive," she said. "Do you really think that will be any better?"

He glared at her. "Shut up. I'm done talking to you." He turned away, a gesture that struck her as childish.

She took the opportunity to study the room more closely. There were no windows, no openings of any kind, other than the door he was sitting in front of. She mentally reviewed the equipment in her backpack that might be used as a weapon. She had a pair of angled bandage scissors, but they wouldn't be much defense against a real weapon, like a knife or gun.

Maybe the hostage negotiator really would talk him into surrendering, or at least letting her go. For all his bravado, Carl struck her as a weak man. Weak enough to allow his sister to talk him into what seemed to her a very flawed plan. Had Melissa really believed it would work? Or did she have some other motive for putting her brother—and her daughter— in such danger?

BRANDON SHEFFIELD HELD his daughter on his lap in the back seat of a sheriff's department SUV, one arm around her, relief in every line of his face. Melissa sat by his side, smiling at the girl. "We need to ask Dawn a few questions," Travis said as he and Erik approached the open door of the vehicle.

"We need to get her to a doctor," Brandon said. "She's burning up with fever."

"This will only take a few minutes," Travis said. "And she's the only one who can give us the information we need."

"Just a few questions," Brandon said. "You can save the rest for when she's better."

Travis squatted beside the open door. "Hello, Dawn," he said. "I'm Sheriff Walker. Did your uncle Carl say where he planned to go next?"

Dawn leaned in closer to her father. "He said he wanted to go to Mexico, because it's warm there."

"Did he mention anything else? Did he say why he came here?"

"He said Mama told us to wait here for her."

"Obviously, she's confused," Melissa said. "The poor child is burning up. No one could think clearly in that condition."

Brandon frowned at his wife. "Did Uncle Carl talk to your mother on the phone?" he asked.

"Lots of times," Dawn said. "And Mom came to see us and drove us places." She turned to look at Melissa. "Mama, why did you keep going away? Why didn't you let me come home with you?"

Melissa managed a weak smile. "You're confused, sweetie," she said. "Of course Mama didn't leave you."

Dawn squirmed. "I have to go to the bathroom," she said.

"I'll take you," Melissa opened her car door. "We'll have to go in the woods, but you know how to do that. Then we can leave here and go home."

"Deputy Douglas will go with you," Travis said.

He looked around for Jamie, spotted her and waved her over.

But Melissa hadn't waited. She had hold of Dawn's hand and the two were hurrying toward the trees at the edge of the clearing. "Go after them, Jamie," Travis said to the deputy. "Make sure Melissa doesn't try anything."

"Are you going to arrest my wife?" Brandon asked.

"She's admitted she helped her brother carry out this plan to extort money from you," Travis said. "We'll need to take her into custody."

"I can't believe she'd do something like that," Brandon said, his face slack. He didn't sound angry. Erik thought that would come later. For now he was in shock, his world turned upside down.

"You should consult an attorney," Erik said.

Brandon nodded. "I'll find a good criminal defense lawyer to represent Melissa."

"You should find an attorney to represent yourself and your daughter," Erik said.

Brandon's eyes met his, clarity flashing beneath the shock. He nodded. "You're right. I will."

Jamie jogged toward them, Dawn in her arms. She stopped before them, out of breath. "Dawn came out of the woods," Jamie said. "But Mrs. Sheffield didn't."

Chapter Fifteen

"Why hasn't that hostage negotiator called?" Carl stared at his phone. "Don't they realize they have to deal with me?"

"Maybe you could call them," Sheri said. "Or call your sister. Ask her what's going on."

He nodded and punched in a number. Sheri could hear the ringing, then a man's voice answered. "Hello, Carl."

"Who is this? What are you doing with Mel's phone?"

"Mel isn't here." Sheri recognized Erik's voice and felt a surge of, if not relief, a lessening of her anxiety. Erik was very good at his job. He was going to do everything in his power to keep her safe. To keep everyone safe. "She took Dawn into the woods to use the bathroom and apparently decided to run away," Erik said. "She left you to deal with this on your own, Carl."

"No! She wouldn't do that. You're lying to try to get me to cooperate."

"I'm not lying," Erik said. "Melissa is gone. She told us that this was all your fault. You were the one who came up with the idea of kidnapping your niece and asking Brandon to pay a big ransom, and Melissa only helped because you threatened her."

"That's not true!" Carl moaned and hugged his arm across his stomach, nearly bent double. "This was Melissa's idea. She told me it would be easy. Brandon would never know it was me. No one would suspect me. She said she could convince Dawn not to say anything. She set up the offshore account for the ransom and everything. She said it would only take a few hours."

"It's been a lot more than a few hours," Erik said.

"Mel told me she would take care of it!" Carl's voice rose. "I wanted to stop after that first night, but she told me she would fix everything if I was patient."

"Why did you decide to hide up here in that equipment shed?" Erik asked.

"I didn't decide. Mel told me I had to wait here. She dropped us off this morning and said she would be back in a few hours."

"That's not the story she's telling, Carl," Erik said. "If you want to clear this up, you need to release Sheri and come out and talk to us."

"Then you'll arrest me."

"We'll take you to the sheriff's department and you can contact a lawyer to help you."

"Trying to pay for a lawyer is what got me into this mess in the first place!"

"All right. Calm down. It's going to be okay. Let me talk to Sheri."

"No."

"I want to make sure she's all right."

"I'm fine," Sheri called, hoping Erik would hear her.

"Shut up," Carl said. He punched the button to end the call and threw the phone across the room. It hit the wall hard, the screen shattering.

Sheri stared at the damaged phone. "What are you going to do if they want to talk to you again?" she asked.

"I'm done talking." He sank to the floor and buried his face in his hands. "I'm a dead man," he said. "They'll send me to jail for the rest of my life for this. I can't survive in prison. There are murderers and rapists and really dangerous people in there. They'll eat me alive."

Sheri scooted closer. "If you don't get out there and tell your story, they'll only have Melissa's side of things to go on," she said. "Melissa is putting all the blame on you. That's not right."

He raised his head, tears streaming down his face. "They won't believe me," he said. "They'll believe Melissa. She's beautiful and smart and rich. She gets away with things. She always has." He reached to his side and pulled out the gun.

Sheri drew back. "What are you doing with that?"

He looked at the weapon in his hand. "I didn't want to do this, but I'm already in so deep I don't think it matters." He pointed the pistol at her. "If I hold this to your head and stand in the door of this building, do you think they'll let me go free?"

She stared in horror—at the gun, and then at the hand that held it, a hand that shook, ever so slightly. "That isn't a good idea, Carl," she said.

His free hand lashed out and took hold of her. "It's the only idea I've got."

ERIK HIT THE redial button on Melissa's phone, but no one answered. He looked around, hoping to spot the hostage negotiator his bosses had promised to send, but so far she hadn't shown. The whole side of the mountain was lit up with portable lights, teams of law enforcement officers swarming the area, searching for Melissa Sheffield or waiting for orders on how to deal with Carl Westover.

Brandon and Dawn, escorted by a victim's advocate from the county, had left, on their way to the emergency room to have Dawn examined. Erik had been on his way to the sheriff's SUV to place Melissa's phone in an evidence bag when Carl had called. He had tried to keep the kidnapper talking as long as possible, hoping that word of his sister's betrayal would spur him to want to come out and present his own version of events. But it had only ended up making him angry.

He spotted Travis, phone to his ear, several hundred yards away. Gage was with him, both standing with their backs to the equipment shed. Erik moved out of the reach of the lights, to the back side of the building where Carl was holed up with Sheri. Crusted snow crunched under his feet, but he was confident the constant hum of machinery in the building would prevent anyone inside from hearing his approach. Constructed of cinder blocks painted dark brown, the flat-roofed shed had no windows or back door. The only opening was a louvered vent that was too small for an adult to squeeze through.

He crept up to the back wall and put his ear to the vent, but all he heard was the hum of machinery. He straightened, and pulled his coat more tightly around him. It was even colder here in the darkness, morning still several hours away. Was Melissa regretting her choice of footwear about now? Her high-heeled boots weren't made for fleeing through snowy woods, and how did she expect to reach safety with so many law enforcement personnel searching for her?

People did all kinds of desperate things when they were cornered, he knew. He had known criminals who ate evidence, one who jumped into an ice-cold lake and attempted to swim away, and one who insisted he suffered a split personality and didn't have any idea why all these officers were pointing their guns at him. Sometimes the desperate moves even paid off—the lake swimmer had made it all away across the lake and into a nearby town before he was caught shoplifting from a store. The local cops who arrested him had no idea they were dealing with a dangerous felon until Erik and a fellow agent showed up.

He stepped back from the building and studied it again. They were never going to get in there using force. They would have to find a way to persuade Carl to come out. He returned to the front of the building and found Travis. "Any sign of that negotiator?" the sheriff asked.

"Let me check." Erik pulled out his phone and saw that he had a text. He read it and swore. "The negotiator made it to Eagle Mountain, but then she got lost on some back road and ran out of gas. She's waiting for a deputy to pick her up—as soon as he figures out where she is, since she doesn't know." He stuffed the phone back into his pocket. "Looks like we're on our own. And Carl isn't answering his phone." He related his brief conversation with the kidnapper. "We're going to have to find a way to force him out," Erik concluded.

"I'll get in touch with the satellite company and see about shutting down their equipment," Travis said. "Once it starts to get cold in there, Carl might feel differently about moving to a nice warm cell."

"Right." Of course, anything they did to Carl, Sheri would suffer as well. But Erik knew she was tough. She wouldn't complain about a little cold or hunger if it resulted in her freedom. Though he was definitely going to have a few things to say about her putting herself in danger the way she had—right after he kissed her breathless.

Travis left to find a quieter place to make his call. Gage joined Erik. "We've got a sniper focused on the door," he said. "If Carl comes out with Sheri, the sniper will try to get a clear shot at just Carl."

Erik's stomach flipped at the idea of a bullet anywhere near Sheri. He forced the thought away. "Let's hope it doesn't come to that."

Travis returned. "The satellite company has agreed to cooperate, but it will take a bit to get everything ready to shut down," he said. "In the meantime, I'm going to try talking to Carl. Do you have his number?"

Erik consulted Melissa's phone and read off the number. Travis punched it in and they waited, the buzzing ring loud in the sudden stillness. Travis hung up on the twelfth ring. "I didn't hear any ringing in there," Gage said, and nodded toward the building.

"Those cinder block walls are pretty thick," Erik said. "And with the machinery running, I don't think you could hear anything."

"The machinery should be shutting down any minute now," Travis said. He and Gage discussed the positioning of various deputies while Erik stared at the door of the building. What was going on in there? What if Carl wasn't as nonviolent and passive as everyone believed? What if he tried to hurt Sheri, just when the two of them had found each other again?

Silence descended like a hammer as the machinery in the building abruptly shut off. Travis raised a hand to his mouth. "Carl! This is Sheriff Travis Walker. You are surrounded. Open the door and throw out your weapon!"

Erik held his breath, ears straining. No answer came. No sign of movement. Were Carl and Sheri still in there? Still alive?

Pop! Pop! The shots sounded small and almost innocent, like a cap pistol or a firecracker, but Erik almost doubled over from the pain in his chest as he recognized the gunfire for what it was. "Sheri!" The shout tore from his throat and he staggered toward the building.

Gage wrapped him up in a bear hug and dragged him back, even as the door to the building swung open. Everyone froze.

"It's okay!" Sheri called. "I'm okay. But Carl…" Her voice broke. "Carl isn't okay."

Erik broke free of Gage's grip and ran to her, arriving in time to catch her as she sagged. They clung together, her face buried against his shoulder. "I thought he was going to shoot me," she whispered. "Instead, he shot himself."

He looked past her, to where Carl lay crumpled on the concrete floor, then a tide of law enforcement personnel swept past them. He moved out of the way, taking Sheri with him.

"What happened?" Travis asked the question, standing at Erik's shoulder.

Sheri straightened, and swiped at her tear-stained

cheeks. "He was very upset when he learned his sister had deserted him. He said the situation was hopeless. When he took out the gun, I thought he intended to kill me, but then he… He shot himself." Fresh tears welled. Erik gripped her hand.

"We'll need a statement," Travis said. "While it's still fresh in your mind."

"Of course." She sniffed, then took the handkerchief Erik handed her. "How is Dawn?"

"She's fine. She's with her father, who was taking her to be checked out by a doctor."

"That's good." She dabbed at her eyes. "Did Melissa really run away?"

"She did," Travis said. "But we'll find her." He looked at Erik. "Take her to the station. Someone there can take her statement. Then take her home."

"I need a vehicle," Erik said.

Travis dug out his keys and tossed them to Erik. "I'll get a ride back with Gage."

Erik led Sheri to the SUV and helped her into the front seat. But instead of moving to the driver's seat, he leaned over her. "Don't you ever do anything like that again," he said, his voice rough. "When I heard those shots, I thought I was going to die."

She pressed her palm to his cheek. "You would have done the same thing—to save that little girl. I know you would have."

"I'm a cop," he said. "That's part of the job."

"And I was a mother. That's part of my job, too.

It doesn't matter that Dawn wasn't my child. I had to protect her."

They leaned in, foreheads pressed together. "I love you," he said. "Even at the worst times, before the divorce, I still loved you. I just couldn't figure out how to live with you and my grief, too."

"I know." She pressed her lips to his, a brief, soft kiss. "I love you, too."

"I want to try again," he said. "I think we belong together."

"Yes." Another kiss. "We're stronger now. I think we can do this."

He wrapped his arms around her and dragged her to him, and kissed her with a fierceness born of fear of losing her and joy at having her restored to him. It was a very long time before they pulled apart, and longer still before he moved out of her arms and around to the driver's seat, to finish out the rest of what had to be done on this long night.

Epilogue

A week after the showdown on Marietta Peak, the sheriff contacted Erik and asked him to stop by the office. "I thought you would want an update on the case and I prefer to do it in person," Travis said.

When Erik showed up with Sheri in tow, the sheriff fixed his gaze on the diamond ring on the third finger of Sheri's left hand and said, "I take it the rumors are true that you're going to be staying in town?"

"I'm being transferred to the Junction office, effective immediately," Erik said.

"Erik and I are getting married," Sheri said, somewhat unnecessarily, Erik thought, since everyone in town seemed to be aware of the news, judging by the chorus of congratulations the two of them received wherever they went.

Travis nodded. "Congratulations."

"Is that what you wanted to see me about?" Erik asked.

"No. I wanted to let you know Colorado State Patrol picked up Melissa Sheffield this morning."

Sheri gasped. "Where?" She flushed. "That is, if you're allowed to tell me."

"She was buying gas at a store in Trinidad, near the New Mexico state line," Travis said. "A clerk recognized her picture from the news stories. She's being held there and will be transported to Junction tomorrow."

"That's a relief," Sheri said. "I didn't like the idea of her running free."

"We're still pulling together the case against her, but I doubt she'll be free again for a very long time," Travis said.

"Here's one more thing you can add to your files." Erik handed over a thin folder. "I just received this this morning as well. It's a report from the FBI on the numbered account Brandon was instructed to wire the ransom money to. Melissa set it up in Carl's name, but what Carl probably didn't know was that she had also set up a second account in her own name. Anything deposited in the first account would be automatically transferred to the second."

"She was picked up with a forged passport and an airline ticket to Buenos Aires," Travis said.

"I think she planned this all along," Erik said. "If Brandon had paid out the cash, Melissa would have found a way to have Carl identified as the kidnapper. She would have unspooled her story about being forced to help him and he would have been arrested and sent to prison. After a suitable amount of time, she would have disappeared to Buenos Aires or some point beyond, with a new identity and a million dollars to smooth the way."

"I almost feel sorry for Carl," Sheri said.

"Don't," Erik said. "He knew what his sister was like, but he let greed get the better of his judgment."

"Sheriff, there's someone here to see you," Adelaide interrupted them. "All of you." She turned and motioned to someone down the hall.

A moment later, Dawn Sheffield appeared in the doorway, her father close behind. "Hello!" Sheri smiled and leaned toward the little girl. "It's good to see you again."

Dawn looked like a different child now, pink-cheeked and smiling, her long brown hair pulled back from her face. She wore jeans and a pink sweater and a pink parka and white snow boots. "I made you this," she said, and thrust an envelope at Sheri.

"We were going to stop by the school after this," Brandon said. "We didn't expect to find you here."

"I made this, too," Dawn said, and handed Travis another envelope.

Sheri opened her envelope and took out a card with a drawing of colorful cliffs in blue and white and green, a tiny figure perched near the top of one cliff. "That's you, climbing the ice," Dawn said. "I watched you before…well, before everything happened."

"It's perfect." Sheri's eyes shone. She reached out and pulled Dawn to her. "Thank you so much. I'll treasure this."

"Thank you," Dawn said. She took a deep breath.

"I know Uncle Carl let me go because you offered to take my place."

"Your uncle loved you," Sheri said. "He never would have hurt you."

Dawn nodded, and turned to the sheriff. "Thank you to you and all your officers, too," she said.

"You're very welcome." Travis stood his card, which showed a mountain with a tower at the top and several men and women with big stars on their chests.

"How are you doing?" Erik asked Brandon.

"Okay." Brandon nodded. "It's been tough, but Dawn and I are seeing a family therapist and I've consulted attorneys." He glanced at Travis. "The sheriff shared that Carl's accomplice was apprehended earlier today. I have a lot of mixed feelings about all of this, but we'll get through it." He patted his daughter's shoulder. "Dawn and I are headed back to Denver today. We just wanted to stop by and say thank you again for everything."

"We'll keep you posted," Travis said. "Stop by anytime you're in town."

"I've already listed the house," Brandon said. "Too many bad memories there for both of us. I think we'll get a new place. Someplace the two of us can make a fresh start."

They left and Erik and Sheri followed them out. In the car, Sheri admired the card once more. "I hope she'll be all right," she said. "That's a lot to go through at such a young age. At any age, really."

"Her father will help her," Erik said. "They'll help

each other." He took her hand and squeezed it. "I like what he said, about fresh starts."

"Yes." She turned her palm up and laced her fingers with his. "Are we really going to do this and not screw up?"

"We're going to be a family again." He glanced at her. "I always wanted more children, didn't you?"

Her smile pierced him, full of joy and pain and hope. "Yes. I'd like that. The idea terrifies me, but I still want to try."

"So much of life is terrifying like that," he said. "But you know how to be brave. You've done it for years." He kissed her knuckles. "We'll be brave together this time." The wedding vows would mean even more when he said them this time. Now he knew the cost of all he had given away before. Now that they were together again, they were never going to let each other go.

* * * * *

Look for the next book in Cindi Myers's Eagle Mountain Search and Rescue miniseries in January!

And if you missed the first book in the series, you can find Eagle Mountain Cliffhanger *wherever Harlequin Intrigue books are sold!*

COMING NEXT MONTH FROM

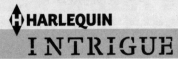

HARLEQUIN
INTRIGUE

#2115 LAWMAN TO THE CORE
The Law in Lubbock County • by Delores Fossen
When an intruder attacks Hallie Stanton and tries to kidnap the baby she's adopting, her former boss, ATF agent Nick Brodie, is on the case. But will his feelings for Hallie and her son hinder his ability to shut down a dangerous black market baby ring?

#2116 DOCKSIDE DANGER
The Lost Girls • by Carol Ericson
To protect his latest discovery, FBI agent Tim Ruskin needs LAPD homicide detective Jane Falco off the case. But when intel from the FBI brass clashes with the clues Jane is uncovering, Tim's instincts tell him to put his trust in the determined cop, peril be damned.

#2117 MOUNTAIN TERROR
Eagle Mountain Search and Rescue • by Cindi Myers
A series of bombings have rocked Eagle Mountain, and Deni Traynor's missing father may be the culprit. SAR volunteer Ryan Welch will help the vulnerable schoolteacher unearth the truth. But will the partnership lead them to their target...or something more sinister?

#2118 BRICKELL AVENUE AMBUSH
South Beach Security • by Caridad Piñeiro
Mariela Hernandez has a target on her back, thanks to her abusive ex-husband's latest plot. Teaming up with Ricky Gonzalez and his family's private security firm is her only chance at survival. With bullets flying, Ricky will risk it all to be the hero Mariela needs.

#2119 DARK WATER DISAPPEARANCE
West Investigations • by K.D. Richards
Detective Terrence Sutton is desperate to locate his missing sister—one of three women who recently disappeared from Carling Lake. The only connection to the crimes? A run-down mansion and Nikki King, the woman Terrence loved years ago and who's now back in town...

#2120 WHAT IS HIDDEN
by Janice Kay Johnson
Jo Summerlin's job at her stepfather's spectacular limestone cavern is thrown into chaos when she and former navy SEAL Alan Burke discover a pile of bones and a screaming stranger. Have they infiltrated a serial killer's perfect hiding place?

**YOU CAN FIND MORE INFORMATION ON UPCOMING HARLEQUIN TITLES,
FREE EXCERPTS AND MORE AT HARLEQUIN.COM.**

HICNM1122

Get 4 FREE REWARDS!

We'll send you 2 FREE Books plus 2 FREE Mystery Gifts.

FREE
Value Over
$20

Both the **Harlequin Intrigue®** and **Harlequin® Romantic Suspense** series feature compelling novels filled with heart-racing action-packed romance that will keep you on the edge of your seat.

YES! Please send me 2 FREE novels from the Harlequin Intrigue or Harlequin Romantic Suspense series and my 2 FREE gifts (gifts are worth about $10 retail). After receiving them, if I don't wish to receive any more books, I can return the shipping statement marked "cancel." If I don't cancel, I will receive 6 brand-new Harlequin Intrigue Larger-Print books every month and be billed just $6.24 each in the U.S. or $6.74 each in Canada, a savings of at least 14% off the cover price or 4 brand-new Harlequin Romantic Suspense books every month and be billed just $5.24 each in the U.S. or $5.99 each in Canada, a savings of at least 13% off the cover price. It's quite a bargain! Shipping and handling is just 50¢ per book in the U.S. and $1.25 per book in Canada.* I understand that accepting the 2 free books and gifts places me under no obligation to buy anything. I can always return a shipment and cancel at any time by calling the number below. The free books and gifts are mine to keep no matter what I decide.

Choose one: ☐ **Harlequin Intrigue**   ☐ **Harlequin Romantic Suspense**
　　　　　　　　 Larger-Print　　　　　　　　　　(240/340 HDN GRCE)
　　　　　　　　 (199/399 HDN GRA2)

Name (please print)

Address　　　　　　　　　　　　　　　　　　　　　　　　　　　　Apt. #

City　　　　　　　　　　　State/Province　　　　　　　　　　Zip/Postal Code

Email: Please check this box ☐ if you would like to receive newsletters and promotional emails from Harlequin Enterprises ULC and its affiliates. You can unsubscribe anytime.

Mail to the Harlequin Reader Service:
IN U.S.A.: P.O. Box 1341, Buffalo, NY 14240-8531
IN CANADA: P.O. Box 603, Fort Erie, Ontario L2A 5X3

Want to try 2 free books from another series? Call 1-800-873-8635 or visit www.ReaderService.com.

*Terms and prices subject to change without notice. Prices do not include sales taxes, which will be charged (if applicable) based on your state or country of residence. Canadian residents will be charged applicable taxes. Offer not valid in Quebec. This offer is limited to one order per household. Books received may not be as shown. Not valid for current subscribers to the Harlequin Intrigue or Harlequin Romantic Suspense series. All orders subject to approval. Credit or debit balances in a customer's account(s) may be offset by any other outstanding balance owed by or to the customer. Please allow 4 to 6 weeks for delivery. Offer available while quantities last.

Your Privacy—Your information is being collected by Harlequin Enterprises ULC, operating as Harlequin Reader Service. For a complete summary of the information we collect, how we use this information and to whom it is disclosed, please visit our privacy notice located at corporate.harlequin.com/privacy-notice. From time to time we may also exchange your personal information with reputable third parties. If you wish to opt out of this sharing of your personal information, please visit readerservice.com/consumerschoice or call 1-800-873-8635. **Notice to California Residents**—Under California law, you have specific rights to control and access your data. For more information on these rights and how to exercise them, visit corporate.harlequin.com/california-privacy.

HIHRS22R2

HARLEQUIN
PLUS

Announcing a **BRAND-NEW** multimedia subscription service for romance fans like you!

Read, Watch and Play.

Experience the easiest way to get the romance content you crave.

Start your **FREE 7 DAY TRIAL** at
<u>www.harlequinplus.com/freetrial</u>.

HARPLUS0822